Match

Three Tails
H. L. Burke

For information about H. L. Burke's latest novels, to sign up for the author's monthly newsletter, or to contact the writer, go to
www.hlburkeauthor.com
and sign up for the author's newsletter!
Free eBook for Newsletter Subscribers!

Copyright © 2019 H. L. Burke
All rights reserved.
Cover Design by Jennifer Hudzinski
Whisker Width was originally published in the *Paws, Claws, and Magic Tales* Anthology.

To All the Cats I've Loved.

~Heidi

Cap Plays Cupid

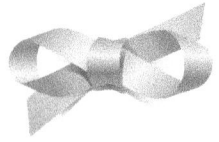

Chapter One

The day my human tried to put a tiny bow tie on me was the day I realized how very much she needed a boyfriend.

But let me start a little before that. My name is Captain Rogers. My human says she named me this because I have the most beautiful blue eyes, just like a certain star-spangled fellow she's obsessed with. She's wrong, of course. She's shown me said Captain's eyes multiple times, and his aren't nearly as blue, or as beautiful, as mine. Still, he's apparently her favorite thing aside from me, so I'll let him have a pass on the "not quite as pretty" eyes thing.

Where was I? Oh yes. For the most part my human just calls me Cap. I'm five-years-old, and I've been with Missy for all but six months of that. Before that, it was mostly "the place with the cages." I didn't like the place with the cages all that much. It smelled like dog, and you could hear them barking in the distance. I still get nervous when I hear barking dogs. I think they call that PTSD ... Pet Traumatic Something Dogs.

Anyway, I'm an impressive specimen (my vet said so, and though I'm not terribly fond of him, he's right), with white fur except for my two ginger ears and my ginger tail. Missy is also a superior specimen, in my not so humble opinion. She's got reddish curls and freckles that match the spots on my nose almost perfectly. Even better, she works from our apartment in a job that requires a lot of sitting, so her lap is almost always available. It's a nice lap. Easily in my top three places to sleep (right after the beam of sun that comes in from the bedroom window and the top of the refrigerator.).

I don't like to brag (actually, I love it. Who am I kidding?), but I'm the most important thing in Missy's life. She's always liked to draw, but once she got me, she found her true calling in life: drawing me. Now she spends all day drawing cartoons of me and posting them on the internet. Apparently people buy t-shirts and stickers and coffee mugs with me on them. I'm kind of big deal. She does some other design work on the side, but pictures of me are the best, just like I'm the best. Missy said so. Missy should know. Missy is an artist and the best human in the world. I love Missy.

The day of the bow tie incident, I was dozing in Missy's lap. Her left hand stroked my back while her right hand did the drawing work. The pencil scratched pleasantly against the paper, a sound I quite like. I twitched my ears trying to hear it better.

When her phone went off literally inches from my listening ears, I jerked and hit my head on the edge of her desk.

"Dangit!" Missy hissed. I peeked over the desk and found her picture marred by a sharp line where her pencil had jolted away from the adorable image of me snoozing on top of a laptop keyboard. "Why can't people just email?" Missy grumbled. Missy didn't get a lot of phone calls.

Yawning, I sat up and bumped my head against her chin, comforting her as the phone continued to ring. As far as I was concerned, she didn't need to give that silly phone the time of day. Not when she'd been so content and happy, petting and drawing me moments before. If I could've told her this, she probably never would've answered, but communicating with humans is a bit of a lost cause. She set the phone on the desk beside her drawing, pushed the speaker button, and said, "Hello, this is Missy."

"Hey, Miss, it's me, Dana!"

My ears flattened at the sound of the familiar yet unwelcome voice. Dana was a long-time "friend" of Missy's. She came over every few weekends, took up the best chair in the apartment, and made fussy noises like "shoo, shoo!" if I came in her general direction. I didn't like Dana much, but Missy, for whatever reason, seemed to tolerate her.

"Oh, hi, Dan." Missy's shoulders slumped. Maybe she didn't feel much like tolerating Dana today.

"I got your RSVP today." Dana's voice continued to shriek from the phone as Missy picked up her eraser and rubbed out the unwanted line from her drawing.

"Cool. Looking forward to the wedding," Missy replied, though her nose wrinkled when she said it.

"Yes, well, that's why I'm calling. You didn't check the box for a plus one."

Missy cringed. "So?"

"Well, if you don't have a date, you should've called me! Haven't I always been able to set you up on short notice? I've got a whole list of eligible bachelors. Tom's cousin is single—and a lawyer."

"I'd really just rather not bother with it." Missy rubbed my ears. "It's your big day, after all. Don't worry about me. It's not like I was planning to dance."

"Yes, but Dominic—that's Tom's cousin—he's really cute. Marathon runner—"

"Really, Dana, I don't need you to set me up. I'm not in the market right now. I've got a lot going on in my life—"

Dana's snort echoed through the phone's speaker. Missy's fingers gripped into my fur in a way that made me tense.

"Oh, come on, Miss! All you've got going on are your drawings and your cat. You can't bring a cat as your plus one."

"He'd probably be better company for me than Mr. Lawyer Boy." Missy scowled. "It's not that I don't know how to get a date. I just don't want a date right now."

"Oh, don't be ridiculous. Every woman wants a date. If you know how to get one, fine. I'll mark you down for a plus one, but if you don't tell me the name of the man you're inviting by next Tuesday, I'm going to call Dominic on your behalf and make sure he's at your table! You know it's because I love you!"

Missy flushed. "I don't think—"

"After all, your cat won't live forever. You don't want to end up alone, standing over a mass grave of furry friends."

Missy went rigid, and my fur stood on end. What the catnip! If Dana had been in the room, I would've scratched her.

"Buh-bye now!" The phone went silent.

For a moment Missy sat, gaping at the phone. My tail twitched uncontrollably at the base of my spine. How dare that awful woman insinuate that I wouldn't live forever, that I wouldn't always be there for Missy, that Missy needed some man to complete her when she had *me*. It was ridiculous. Missy had to know it was ridiculous.

Snatching up the phone, Missy leaped to her feet sending me spiraling to the carpet.

I landed on all fours, of course. It wasn't as if I was in any danger. Still, my heart jumped. It wasn't like Missy to just get up when I was comfortable. I've actually done some experiments to see how long she'll put up with me on her lap before forcing me to move. Unless bathroom trips are involved, her limit is upwards of three hours. Now, however, she stomped into the other room as if I wasn't even there.

Shaking myself off, I licked my fore-paws before following her to the tiny bedroom. The closet door slammed shut, and she tossed a satin monstrosity in a crinkly plastic bag onto the bed. I hopped up and gave it a sniff. Not particularly great for sleeping on. I hoped she'd move it before nap time.

"And to think I bought a dress for that ditz's wedding."

I jumped out of the way, dodging a pair of high-heeled shoes that landed on top of the dress.

"I should sell the dress and skip her stupid wedding. No! I'll go, but come in my pajamas! My cat pajamas!" She sat beside the clothing items in a huff.

Wanting to deescalate the situation so that she could get back to her quiet afternoon of sitting, drawing, and petting me, I did what I do best.

I was adorable.

I rubbed up against her. Rumbling purrs rose from my throat. I walked across her lap and flicked her nose with my majestic tail. She grunted and rubbed at my back, far too absent-mindedly in my opinion. Obviously her heart and thoughts were elsewhere. Somewhat peeved, I let out a "Meerow?"

She smiled down at me. "I wish I could bring you as my plus one. You'd be the handsomest man at the wedding. Yes, you would!" She bent closer, and I stood on my hind legs to touch my nose to hers. "In fact." She inhaled sharply and stood up again.

I rolled onto the mattress. What was with all the abrupt rising today? Not seeming to notice that she'd knocked me off her lap for the second time in five minutes, Missy rushed to her dresser. At the top of it sat a teddy bear she'd gotten for her last birthday. The bear wore a tiny bow tie which she ripped over its fuzzy head. I twitched my whiskers. What was she up to?

Before I could react, Missy popped the elastic band of the bow tie over my head and straightened it beneath my chin. My claws gripped into the mattress. Every nerve in my sensitive body prickled. What *was* this? Uncertain as to what other course to take, I meowed piteously.

Missy burst out laughing. "You ... you look ... so handsome ..." She pulled her phone from her pocket and snapped a picture of me while I stood, stunned. Missy collapsed on the bed, giggling.

It took several moments of pawing and wriggling to dislodge the bow tie. It finally snapped over my ears and flew onto the bed beside where Missy now lay, still laughing. Frustrated, I shook my body from nose tip to tail tip before sitting down to wash my ears. The elastic band from the bow tie had rumpled them ever so slightly, and it would take a lot of work to get them "just so" again.

However, before I was half done, Missy's giggles and snorts turned to full on shrieking.

Concerned at this erratic behavior, I put my paw on her arm. She rolled over to face me. Her laughter grew hysterical, her face puckering until I wasn't sure if she were going to sneeze or scream. It was then that I noticed tears streaming down her face.

Missy was crying? Why was Missy crying? Was it because I didn't want to wear the stupid bow tie? I pushed myself under her chin and rubbed and purred and flirted with all my might.

Stop crying, Missy. I'm here! I'm here! Don't cry!

Missy gripped me in a suffocating hug, but continued to sob. Her tears seeped through my fur. Her hold made it difficult to breathe. Still, I owed it to Missy, the one who had saved me from the place with the cages, my favorite lap, the giver of treats and pets, to be there, to let her complete this strange human ritual of tears. Uncertain what to do, I licked her face.

Tears actually are rather tasty. Wet, of course, but with a pleasant hint of salt that I rather liked. Finding this not the most unpleasant of ways to comfort her, I continued to groom her face, until her tears calmed and she started laughing again.

"Oh, Cap, you sweet, sweet boy." Sitting up, she held me at arm's length. "You don't need to make out with me, though I appreciate the effort."

I wriggled a bit. Humans could be so awkward in their displays of affection.

She let out a long breath. "I need to stand up to Dana. I really do. I mean, she's got a whole wedding to plan. You'd think she'd have better things to do than to bully her college roommate into dating some random in-law." She set me down.

The mention of Dana set my whiskers twitching again. Unable to express my contempt for that awful human, I instead nudged one of Missy's high heels off the bed. It landed on the floor with a pleasing "thunk." Satisfied, I batted at the second, but Missy grabbed it right before it toppled. I sniffed, but looked in the other direction, not wanting her to see how disappointed I was to be denied a second "thunk."

Missy fondled my ears. Slightly assuaged, I leaned into it. She sighed, staring right past me in a way that made me suspect she wasn't quite comforted yet. I increased the volume of my purrs, hoping to calm her.

"I shouldn't have let her get to me, Cap, but you know, I lied. I don't know how to get a date. I mean, don't get me wrong, I love my life. I love my job. I love my apartment. I love you. Oh, I love you so much." She pressed her cheek against mine. I arched my back to fully immerse myself in the nuzzling. "But sometimes, I just wish I had someone to talk to about the latest Marvel movie or to hold my hand … so I didn't have to go to the theater alone. Maybe someone I could be the Agent Carter for, you know?"

I didn't. I mean, I vaguely knew those were things she liked, but I liked them only in a "when she watches them she sits still and lets me lick the butter off her popcorn bowl" way.

"I don't *need* a boyfriend." Her mouth formed a firm line. "But dang it, that doesn't mean I don't sometimes want one. Just a little." With another sigh, she picked the dress off the bed and hung it back in the closet. "Maybe Mr. Lawyer-Man wouldn't be so bad." She wandered out of the room.

I considered following but instead sat and thought. My Missy didn't want the Lawyer-Man, but she did want a someone, a Captain, just like me, but maybe more human, able to appreciate movies.

I stuck out my chest. If anyone could solve Missy's problem, it was me. After all, Missy had brought me home from the place with cages. Missy was my everything.

Yes, I was going to find Missy a boyfriend in time for that awful Dana's wedding. In fact, I'd find Missy a boyfriend so awesome that it would make awful Dana jealous. That was what I was going to do.

Unfortunately, I didn't have the slightest idea how.

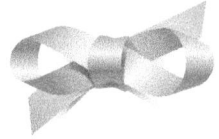

Chapter Two

Our apartment has a large window overlooking the building's parking lot. I mostly use it for pigeon watching (Holy catnip, I *hate* those stupid, strutting pigeons with a fiery passion), but it's also good for people watching on occasion.

When I was in the "place with cages," the cat on the cage to my right was a jaded old street stray with one ear and a nasty attitude. He used to make fun of me when I would wonder what sort of human would take me out of my cage. According to him, all humans look alike, but that's not true. *Most* humans look alike, but any cat who has ever owned a human will tell you that their human is special and unique. If you lined up all the humans in the world, most of them would blur together. Two legs, no fur, no tail, awkward and not really much to look at—but Missy, Missy I'd be able to spot immediately. Missy is my human, and my human is the best human.

So I figured if I looked hard enough at the various humans wandering in and out of our building, I might be able to spot one as special as Missy. From what I've observed of Missy's tastes, I have a general idea what she'll like, enough to know that anything obviously female won't do, neither will the very young or the very old.

Unfortunately, people watching, while less infuriating than pigeon watching (those beady-eyed little ledge demons intentionally taunt me) is also far less intriguing. After what felt like nine lifetimes, my eyes fell shut in spite of my best efforts. However, a cat may sleep, but a cat is never unaware. My ears twitched at every sound. Inside the apartment this consisted mainly of the whir of the printer as Missy made up the latest batch of shipping labels to send pictures of me—and probably a few of other less interesting subjects—all around the world. (I'm kind of a big deal)

Outside, however, the sounds were more sporadic. Every so often a car door would slam in the parking lot or the "beep beep" of automatic locks would alert me to an approaching resident. I'd open one eye just enough to verify that it was an old man, or a woman carrying a toddler, or a fellow walking a dog (I don't need that in my life). Though still determined to find a proper partner for my Missy, my brain couldn't help wandering to other things, like whether that night's supply of Pawsome brand canned cat food would be chicken and liver or seafood medley.

The screech of packing tape sliding over a box jolted me back to present matters. I cast Missy a disapproving glance. She slapped the label on the box.

"When I'm done here, got to head down to the drop box on the corner, okay, Cap? Want to get these in there before the 5 o'clock truck comes by." She placed the box next to a stack of envelopes. "I might stop at that little Chinese place on my way home. Fried shrimp sound good?"

I was on all four paws before you could say "moo goo gai pan." Fried shrimp meant I got to nibble the pinky flesh off the tails she'd toss to the side. Even better than Pawsome brand seafood medley!

"Meow!"

"I thought you'd like that." Missy grinned and put down the tape. "I'll just go slip on my sneakers. You hold down the fort while I'm gone." She crossed to me, scratched under my chin, and headed into the bedroom.

I curled my tail about my paws, thinking wistfully of fried shrimp garnishing a bowlful of seafood medley ... or even better, a can of real tuna.

It was then that a roar like a thousand angry pitbulls sent me rocketing towards the ceiling. I managed to land on the same windowsill I'd launched from. Spine still arched, I whirled to glare out the window. A motorcycle zipped through the parking lot and came to rest in the corner. The rider dismounted and pulled off his black helmet, revealing rippling brown hair on a face that, while not too young, was certainly not too old.

He wore a leather jacket. He rode a motorcycle. Those were things the guy in those movies she liked did, weren't they? I remembered that Missy had kept a picture of that guy on one of those motorcycles as her laptop background for a good two weeks at one point ... before she sensibly returned it to a picture of me sleeping on her bed.

Motorcycle guy ambled towards the entrance to the lobby. How was I going to get him and Missy to meet?

"Okay, my Capsicle." Missy strode out of the backroom wearing her sneakers and a cardigan with a familiar star-spangled logo on it. "I'm off." She propped open the door and turned to grab her stack of packages.

My ears pricked, and before I could think better of it, I bolted from my perch.

"Cap!" Missy wailed as I streaked through her legs and down the hall. "What are you doing?"

Ignoring her, I bee-lined for the staircase. Though I usually only left the apartment in the carrier for my yearly vet trip, I knew the way to the lobby. The question was if I could get there before motorcycle boy disappeared into whatever apartment was his. I had no idea how many people lived in our building, but considering the number of doors I passed just to get to the stairs, and that I knew we were on the third floor, it was unlikely I'd be able to figure out which door was his once he'd disappeared inside it. Thankfully, as I hit the second story landing I saw him, coming up the stairs from the opposite direction. I froze.

Motorcycle boy's gaze never left his phone. He walked right by me, not seeming to notice me or hear the footsteps of Missy pounding down the stairs after me. He turned into the hall and stopped at the second door, fumbling for his keys. I waited just long enough to be sure Missy caught up and saw where I went before darting after motorcycle boy. I zipped over his shoes just as he opened the door.

"What the—?"

Triumphantly, I dashed into his apartment only to skid to a horrified halt.

A vicious little chihuahua, lips curled back to reveal pointy teeth, lunged at me.

Chapter Three

I had just enough presence of mind to make the top of a display case full of shiny gold things in a single bound. The chihuahua hopped up and down beneath me like a demon-possessed pogo stick. His annoying bark grew shriller and more frantic with every leap. Flattening myself into the glass, I hissed at him.

"Lobo! Get away from there!" The door slammed and heavy-booted feet tramped towards me and Mr. Barky McBiteypants. Ignoring the orders of Motorcycle Boy, McBiteypants—Lobo, I guess—skittered in circles, yipping, yapping, and snarling.

Pressed into the case, ears flattened, tail bushing uncontrollably, I tried to pep talk myself out of the situation. *Come on, Cap, he's smaller than you. You could send that little creep flying with one swipe of your mighty paw. Pull yourself together for the sake of Missy!*

Still, some instinct gripped me like my mother's teeth on the back of my neck. The barking of dogs echoing through the place with the cages turned my courage to terror and left me quivering at the top of my perch.

"Where did this cat come from?" Motorcycle Boy glared up at me, ignoring the rampaging canine at his feet.

As if in answer, Missy's frantic knocking shook the door. "Excuse me! Please let me in! I think my cat went in there."

Motorcycle Boy's head jerked towards the door. Snatching Lobo off the ground and tucking him securely under his arm, he hurried to open the door for Missy. Red-faced, my human burst into the room.

"Cap!" She extended her arms to me. Longing for this nightmare to be over, I sprang, colliding with her chest and knocking her back into Motorcycle Boy.

"Hey." Motorcycle Boy grinned.

Lobo snapped at me. I whipped my claws across his face. Stupid beast yelped and scrambled out of his owner's arms, leaving a damp stain on Motorcycle Boy's t-shirt. Lobo scurried to hide behind the couch.

Cursing, Motorcycle Boy stepped back, shedding his jacket and shirt immediately.

Missy inhaled sharply. "Uh ... I ... I didn't mean to ... Sorry for the trouble." She buried her face in my fur, obviously trying not to look at the shirtless wonder in front of her. "Cap has never escaped our apartment before. I didn't even think he wanted to leave. I'm not sure what got into him."

"No trouble." Tossing his soiled shirt to the side, Motorcycle Boy offered her his hand. A courteous fellow would've done something to clothe himself first. Even I knew that, and I didn't even wear clothes. I squirmed, forcing Missy to keep both hands on me, leaving none for him.

"My name's Hunter." He didn't seem to be put off by her ignoring his handshake offer. "I moved in like six months ago, but I've never seen you before ... and I'd remember if I had. You new to the building?"

"No, I've actually been here almost six years." She flushed. "I don't get out much."

"Yeah, well who knows their neighbors anymore." He shrugged. "So that's your cat, huh?"

"Yes, this is Cap." She ruffled my ears. Hopefully she wasn't buying this guy's act. He had the nerve to stand there, half-dressed, in front of my human, and he owned a chihuahua. That on its own was a deal breaker.

"Ah, like Captain Morgan? Captain Jack?" He winked.

"Uh, not really. Rogers, actually."

"Oh, not familiar with that one. Though I'd rather know your name than your cat's." He winked again.

My tail twitched uncontrollably.

"Oh, sorry, it's Missy. Missy Nowak. Look, sorry, but I was about to run an errand. Thanks for letting me get my cat. Good-bye!" She darted around Hunter and out the door.

Good girl, Missy!

When we got back to the apartment, Missy shut me in the bedroom while she took the packages out. She didn't have to do that. I'd learned my lesson. I couldn't tell from window shopping whether a guy was Captain material. No, I needed a better system for man hunting. One that let me know ahead of time if they had a fondness for barky, bitey canines.

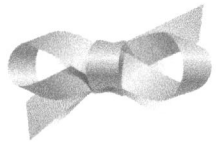

Chapter Four

The problem was I didn't really have a plan B for boyfriend hunting. The apartment had always seemed a wide enough domain, but it had a decided lack of men hanging around it. I knew the men were out there—and some of them had to be smart enough not to own chihuahuas—but how to get to them and figure out if they were good enough for my Missy—well, that was a problem.

Unfortunately, I had bigger worries. Worries that started when Missy brought the cat carrier out of the closet and which intensified as I noticed her watching me out of the corner of her eye throughout the day. I was about to slink off to hide under the bed when the familiar rattle of cat treats sent a thrill through me. I rushed into the kitchenette where she held out a handful of succulent morsels. Enthralled with the tantalizing scent of chicken and liver, I didn't think to run when she scooped me up and barely had time to splay my legs in an attempt to save myself before she'd shoved me into the cat carrier and shut the door.

I whirled about and stared accusingly through the metal grate. How dare she, with all I was doing for her? Then the cage rose and the door to the apartment opened. I cowered on the floor of the carrier as she carried me down the stairs inside it. It was a disconcerting and bouncy ride. By time we reached the lobby, I had resorted to yowling at the top of my voice.

"Shh, sorry boy." Missy put the cage down on the reception desk and gazed in at me.

"Mew?" If she spoke cat, she'd have known how accusatory that mew was ... even not speaking cat, the grimace that passed over her face suggested she knew that she'd betrayed me and that it would take many more chicken and liver flavored treats to make up for this indignity.

"Hey, neighbor!"

My ears flattened against my head as Hunter strolled into the lobby, leading that rat-dog, Lobo, with a camo-patterned leash.

"Oh, hi ... Hunter, right?" Missy turned from me.

Immediately, Lobo burst into frantic yipping.

I hissed as loud as I could.

"Trading in your cat for a better model?" Hunter chuckled at his own "joke."

"No." Missy stuck her chin in the air. "Cap's due for his yearly checkup, is all."

Lobo hopped up and down, trying to get at my cage. Hunter made no attempt to restrain him, but Missy stepped between us.

I gave a low, rumbling "Meow-hiss" in the little beast's general direction.

"He doesn't like the cage much, does he?" Hunter frowned.

"I don't think he likes your dog much." Missy crossed her arms.

"Well, you know what they say about cats and dogs." He winked at her.

"No, what?" From Missy's tone she was about as interested in his response as I was in going to the vet.

"Uh ... well ... they don't like each other much." Hunter's face reddened.

Missy picked up the cage. "Insightful."

My ears perked back up. *I love my human.*

"Excuse me, but I don't want to be late for Cap's appointment. Enjoy your walk!" Missy breezed out of the lobby to a chorus of yapping from the persistent Lobo.

Missy settled me on the passenger seat of her little car. Once the car started moving, I allowed the memory of that annoying pipsqueak and the anxiety over the upcoming vet visit to fade. After all, this was one of the few chances I would have to observe men in their natural habitat and see if I could figure out how to get one for Missy.

A little down the road we stopped for a coffee at a small drive up stand. A human male with blue hair took our order. I considered him for a minute. I hadn't realized humans came in that shade ... however, the pimply state of his skin and the occasional squeak of his voice suggested he might be a little young for my Missy. She sipped her coffee as we drove the last several blocks to the "Healthy Paws Pet Clinic."

Now, I'm rough on vets in general, but I don't mind the one at Healthy Paws so much. We've been going there for four years now, and the vet, an old man with dark skin and white hair, has always made a point to tell Missy how handsome I am. Too old for Missy, but I admired his taste. Maybe he would know someone I could match Missy with.

The receptionist checked us in, and Missy put my cage on the floor as she settled onto the bench. I eyed the other patrons. One was female. Another a man, but elderly—and also there with a golden retriever. I wasn't sure I was up for a life with a dog, even though this one seemed a lot calmer than a pest like Lobo. It lay on the floor at its owner's feet, snoring gently in spite of the location.

"Missy and Cap?" the receptionist called out.

Missy stood. "Here."

"Come with me. We have an exam room ready."

I put up with the vet tech taking my vitals and fawning over me. I'm used to it. Thankfully, Missy didn't put me back in the cage when the vet tech left us alone with a, "The doctor will be with you shortly."

I hopped off the exam table and sniffed around the perimeter. Though the room was spotless, I could still smell a slight trace of the last patient—dog, large breed, I thought. A strand of black fur tickled my nose, and I sneezed just as the door opened.

"Bless you!" Missy and the man in a lab coat said simultaneously. Missy spun to face him, and her jaw dropped. I tilted my head to one side.

"You're not Doctor Govera," Missy stammered.

The man gave a smile that reached to a pair of twinkling blue eyes almost as blue as mine—almost. "No, I'm the new vet here." He pulled up a wheeled stool and flipped the page up on his clipboard. "Started last month, to ease the transition when Doctor G retires this summer. I'm Doctor Spencer."

Missy scooped me up. Her pulse throbbed through her into me. Was she afraid? Was this new doctor a threat? Her fingers ruffled my fur.

"Nice to meet you."

"Why don't you put your boy on the table and let me have a look at him? Says here his name is …" He glanced back down at the clipboard. "Captain?"

"Mostly I call him Cap, but he answers to Capsicle, too."

Doctor Spencer laughed." So, it's Captain *Rogers*. Nice."

Pink tinged Missy's cheeks. "I have a bit of a thing for comic book movies."

"Hey, me too. Look." He stuck out his leg so that his ankle extended beyond the cuff of his khakis, revealing star-spangled socks.

"Awesome!" Missy grinned.

My whiskers twitched. What was happening here? This was my vet appointment, and the vet had barely looked at me … was it just me or was he looking at Missy a lot?

The vet and Missy continued to chat pleasantly as they went over my eating and sleeping habits. The fellow had the nerve to suggest I could lose a few ounces.

"Probably more an issue of lack of exercise than diet. I'm assuming he's exclusively an indoor cat?" The doctor arched an eyebrow.

"Yeah, I mean, I've thought about looking into a cat leash so I can take him for walks."

"That might work, but if you don't want to go through the trouble of leash training him, just whip out a laser pointer a few times a week and tire him out a little." The vet scratched at my chin, and for a moment I forgot that I was trying to dislike him. Then his gaze left me and swept over Missy. I stiffened and flitted to the other end of the examination table to wash my paws.

A thought struck me. Why was I annoyed at this man for taking notice of Missy? Wasn't that exactly what I was looking for? Still, the idea of sharing her with this fellow—I didn't like it. A vet was not an acceptable Captain. A vet might bring home pointy needles and invasive thermometers. A vet would make every day like a check up. No. I would *not* tolerate a vet in Missy's life. She could do so much better.

However, this did mean a hundred percent of the men I'd considered were not right for Missy. Perhaps there wasn't a man out there good enough for Missy. Perhaps this whole "boyfriend" idea was stupid. Missy and I were a team. We didn't need Mr. Smiley-Vet-Man barging in on our life.

Flicking my tail in the doctor's face, I hopped down from the table to paw at the door. Hopefully Missy would get the hint.

The vet stood and cleared his throat. "I guess we're done here ... I mean, unless there are any concerns you have? Questions?"

"No, he's been pretty much himself lately." Missy picked me up and eased me towards the cage. Normally I'd put up a fuss, but I wanted to get away from Vet-Man ASAP.

"Well, he isn't due for his boosters until next year. We'll send a postcard to remind you when that's close." He offered her his hand. "I guess I won't see you until then, though, you know, if you ever need anything, I'm just a phone call away ... or email ... Do you need my card?"

"Yes, that would be nice."

Realizing she intended to dally, I scrambled out of her arms and slipped into the cage to wait. Missy's mouth dropped open.

"Something wrong?" Doctor Spencer tilted his head to one side.

"Uh ... no, it's just he's never ..." She swallowed and took the rectangle of cardboard he offered her. "Thank you. I'll miss Doctor Govera, but he's obviously leaving his patients in excellent hands."

Doctor Spencer rubbed the back of his neck, face reddening. "That's nice of you to—"

"Meerowwwwww!" I let out my most demanding cry.

Missy reached down, fastened my cage shut, and lifted it—with me inside—off the exam room floor. "Sorry, looks like he's eager to get home."

"Yeah, I don't blame him. Well, have a good afternoon."

As Missy carted me out of the exam room, I glared at the doctor through the air holes of my carrier. I wasn't going to let that lab-coat wearing flirt walk off with my human.

No, Missy was mine, and mine alone.

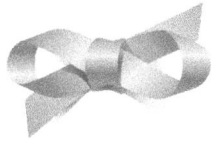

Chapter Five

Though I thought the crisis had been averted, I was wrong. When we reached the apartment, Missy seemed oddly distracted. She set my carrier down on the floor, then walked over to hang up her jacket ... and forgot about me.

After at least two minutes of waiting patiently—far more than would be expected of a lesser cat—I started turning in circles and pawing at the carrier's door. When that failed, I let out my most piteous wail.

"Oh, Cap!" Missy jumped from the couch where she'd been sitting, staring into space, and let me out.

I bounded from the awful cage, shook myself off, and sat to wash my paws.

Without so much as an apology, Missy sank onto the couch again, fingering a slip of cardboard.

The vet's card? Seriously?

What had happened to my vibrant, attentive owner? What had that vet done to her? After all, he was just like any other human male. She'd sent that awful Hunter packing without hesitation—of course, awful Hunter was ... awful. The vet had chatted with her about things she liked, had given proper appreciation to me, had been—nice. As much as I hated to admit it, he was a nice human. Just like my Missy. Had I let my prejudice against vets ruin my human's chances at happiness?

A little repentant, I hopped up next to her and butted my forehead against her cheek.

"Ah, sweet boy," she cooed. Her fingers massaged between my ears, down my neck, and over my spine. My purr rumbled to life like our apartment's heater kicking on during a coldsnap. She tucked the vet's card into her pocket. "Well, we're in for the night, I guess." Her stomach grumbled, and she grimaced. "Dang, I was so worried about making your appointment on time, I didn't stop to get lunch like I'd planned." She glanced at her phone. "Almost six, and all I've had today was that coffee—better get something in my stomach before I pass out." She laughed and started towards the kitchenette.

The doorbell rang.

Missy's brow furrowed. She gazed through the peephole then opened the door a crack. "Hunter?"

My fur stood on end. Sniffing for the stench of chihuahua, I slank to where I could see Hunter smirking through the crack.

"Hey, Miss Missy." He winked.

My ears flattened against my head.

"How did you get my apartment number?" Missy asked.

"The apartment manager. I told him how I rescued your cat yesterday and wanted to check in on you. Nice guy. Knows how to hook a fella up." Again he winked. I sincerely hoped he had something in his eye, because if that was his idea of flirting, he was going to be single—and in Missy's hair—for a long time.

"Oh ... well, I'm fine and Cap's fine. Did you need something?" Her fingers tightened on the door knob.

"Need? Nah, but since we've met and are neighbors and all, I thought I'd be neighborly. I'm having some friends over to watch the game tonight. You want to come by? There'll be pizza."

"What game?"

Hunter's caterpillar eyebrows shot up. "The playoffs?"

"Oh ... baseball, right?"

"No, basketball. Baseball is just starting, not ending."

"I really don't follow sports." She shrugged.

"I can see that." He smirked. "It's cute."

Did he just call Missy *cute*? Wanting to get between him and my human, I bolted for the door. Unfortunately, this had the opposite result.

"Oh, Cap!" Missy snatched me up, releasing the door. It swung further open, allowing Hunter to ease inside. Missy's hold on me tightened.

"Ah, the rascal trying to get out again?" Hunter reached towards my head.

I hissed. He jerked his hand back, eyes widening.

"Kinda bloodthirsty for a kitty cat, isn't he?"

"He's not usually like this." Missy let out a long breath. "Thank you for the invitation, but sports just aren't my thing."

"Doesn't really matter if they're your thing or not. It's still a party. Like I said, there'll be pizza and beer—I can slip to the corner store and grab you some wine coolers if you'd rather."

"I'm still not sure—"

"Oh, come on. It'll be fun. What else are you going to do? Spend the evening drinking with your cat?" He turned away. "You know my apartment number. Game starts at seven. Looking forward to seeing you there." With another wink, he exited the apartment slamming the door behind him.

Missy cursed under her breath and set me down. "Why do people act like spending time with a cat is such a bad thing?" She echoed my thoughts.

I gave a sympathetic meow.

She smiled down at me. "Yeah, you get it, don't you, Capsicle?" I rubbed up against her legs. "You really are my best boy," she whispered. Her face brightened. "Hey, we should have our own party. We don't need Hunter's pizza. I'll order my own. You want some tuna? Feels like a tuna kind of night."

My ears twitched. My whole body tensed as she walked to the kitchenette and opened up a cabinet. Her fingers tickled the rim of a glinting metal can with a tantalizing green wrapper.

Her phone went off.

My tail drooped as she turned away from the tuna and answered the call.

"Oh, hi, Dana."

I sniffed in disgust. Dana's timing was one in a long list of reasons to hate her.

"No, I haven't gotten a date yet, but it's only been a couple of days—wait, let me put you on speaker." Missy pushed the button and put the phone on the kitchen counter. She then reached for the tuna again.

My hero.

"Tom and I are going out tonight, and guess who's here with us?" Dana practically squealed.

Missy rolled her eyes. "Batman?"

"No, silly, it's Dominic! You know Tom's lawyer cousin—"

"Yeah, I vaguely remember you mentioning him." Missy pulled back the tab, releasing the delightful scent of canned fish into the apartment. Though distracted by the phone call—and Dana's jarring voice—I hopped up onto the counter and started to munch.

Ah, sweet, succulent chicken of the sea, how I love you.

Missy absently stroked my fur. "So you just called to tell me you're going out for drinks with Tom's cousin?"

"Not to just tell you! To *invite* you. We're at *The Cape of Good Hops*, that brewery down on Fifth and Elm? If you leave now, you can be here before the appetizers get here. Come on! When you see how Dominic looks in his designer jeans, you'll thank me."

"Does Tom know you're looking at another man's jeans?"

I snickered between gulps of tuna.

"Oh, come on, Missy. Don't be such a stick in the mud. After all, did you really have any plans tonight? Other than hanging out with that silly cat?"

Missy scowled. "Actually, I received an invite to watch the game with a neighbor. A *male* neighbor?"

"Really? He's not like eighty is he? Grandfather types don't count."

"No, I think he's my age-ish."

My claws extended unbidden. Was Missy being serious? Was she considering going to Hunter's? She had to be lying.

"You're lying, aren't you?" Dana accused on cue.

"No! Of course not. His name is Hunter, and he came by and said he was having some friends over and wanted me to come too." Missy stuck her chin in the air, regardless of the fact that Dana couldn't see the defiant expression.

"Huh. Pics or it didn't happen."

"Whatever. Look, I need to feed Cap and get a few things done before I have to go watch the game, all right?"

"Okay, but I'm serious about the pics! Buh-bye, now!"

Missy groaned as the line went dead. She leaned against the refrigerator. "If I don't go to Hunter's now, I'm a liar."

I licked tuna off my whiskers. I didn't care if Missy was a liar. It wasn't like she was lying to me.

"I don't know, Cap. Maybe Dana's right. If I don't put myself out there, if I don't do things out of my comfort zone, how am I ever going to meet *anyone*?" She reached into her pocket and pulled out the vet's card. "Even when I'm interested in someone, when I have a great feeling about them, I don't know what to do about it. What to say. How to stop them from walking in and out of my life like a Stan Lee cameo."

My tail twitched. Was Missy still thinking about Mr. Vet-Man? They'd talked for maybe a half hour, mostly about me. I guess he did have the star-spangled socks, and he did treat me like the impressive specimen I am ... but he was just a human ... just like my Missy was a human. The best human.

Could Mr. Vet-Man be the best human for my best human?

"I need to take charge of my life, do something drastic, different." Missy yanked open the junk drawer, fished around, and pulled out a coin. "Okay, so heads I *head* to Hunter's and watch the game. Tails, I go check out Dominic in his designer jeans. Sounds about right." She laughed but didn't smile.

I leaped from the counter and circled her legs, meowing.

No, Missy! You deserve better than stupid chihuahua man or to be bullied by awful Dana. You deserve a Captain!

Regret boiled in my stomach. Why had I forced her away from Mr. Vet-Man so quickly? She wouldn't have a reason to see him until my next appointment which was ages away ... or unless I got sick.

Missy tossed the coin in the air. With all my might and willpower, I forced the tuna out of my stomach and onto her shoes.

"Cap! What the heck!" Missy staggered back. The coin hit the floor and rolled under the fridge.

Suspecting the vomiting wouldn't be enough, I threw myself onto the floor, paws in the air, and started to twitch.

"Cap!" Missy's voice rose to a wail. "Cap! What's going on?" She knelt beside me and gave me a gentle shake. "Cap, wake up!"

I kept my eyes tightly closed. Yes, it was degrading, but if it got Missy to do what I hoped she'd do, it'd be worth it.

"Hold on, Cap! I'll call the vet ... oh ... they're probably closed. Maybe they have an emergency line... oh Cap." Her words grew teary, but I dared not open my eyes, just lay still. I heard the beeping as Missy dialed. She lay the phone on the floor next to me, her hand over my chest. "Still breathing, good. Oh, Cap, what is going on? You were fine a minute ago?"

"Healthy Paws Clinic, Doctor Spencer speaking. How can I help you?" a familiar voice echoed through the speaker.

"Doctor! You're still there!" Missy gasped.

"Just finishing up some paperwork. Miss ... Nowak? Cap's mom, right?"

"Yes, and it's Cap I'm calling about. He just threw up and now he's lying on the floor ... he's unconscious, I think. Can cats faint?"

"Yes, but there's usually a reason for it. Did he eat anything he shouldn't have?"

"I don't think so. He had some tuna, but he threw that up. I can't wake him up! I don't know what to do."

"Can you bring him in? I'll unlock the door for you."

"You'd do that?"

"Yeah, if he's unconscious, it could be something serious. I want to look him over as soon as possible. Try not to move him more than you have to, but get him down here."

It took all my concentration to remain limp as she shoveled me into the cat carrier, snatched up her keys, and rocketed out the door with me rattling in that stupid cage—but she was going in the right direction for the first time that evening. For that I could take some bruising.

Chapter Six

During the car ride to the vet, it was pretty easy to keep up the charade. Just lie flat on the bottom of the carrier and occasionally give out my most pathetic of meows. The amount of times Missy said, "It's going to be okay, Cap. Hold on, Cap. I'm getting you help, Cap" ... well, that did give me pause. Her voice quavered so pitifully. I got it, I really did. She was afraid of losing me, which had to be terrifying, but still ... it was for her own good.

I hazarded a single eye open as the car stopped, and she leaped out. She opened the passenger door, claimed my carrier, and started towards the door. The flip-sign on the door clearly read 'closed,' and the reception room lights were out, but at her approach, the door opened and heroic Mr. Vet-Man rushed to meet us.

"Is he breathing?" He took the carrier

"I think so," she stammered, peering in through the air holes. I snapped my eyes shut. "He meowed a few times on the drive over."

The door shut behind us. The scent of the various other animals who had been in and out of the vet that day nearly overwhelmed me, but I calmed myself and stayed still.

"What are his symptoms again?" Another door opened and bright light wedged its way under my eyelids. The carrier came to rest.

"First he threw up then he went limp and ... twitchy."

The carrier door creaked open, and a large hand probed my body. I went rigid.

"A seizure?"

"Maybe. I don't know. He's never had one before."

The doctor eased me out of the cage and onto the cold metal of the exam room table.

"And you don't think he ate anything out of the ordinary?"

"I ... I'm not sure, I guess. I mean, we hadn't been home that long."

"Do you have any house plants? Would he have access to cleaners?" The stethoscope pressed into my rib cage.

"No. I've always been really careful about what I allow in the apartment."

"Huh." The vet moved to my tail-end and ... oh, catnip. I've always hated that part. "Temperature's within range. It's odd. His vitals all seem normal."

He pried at my eyelids with his thumb. In spite of my best efforts, I jerked away.

"Huh," he said again.

He slipped his hand under my belly and lifted me a few inches, trying to get me to stand. He let me go, and I immediately flopped onto the table, rolled onto my back, and stuck a paw dramatically in the air for good measure. "I'm honestly not sure what's going on here," Doctor Spencer continued. "Can you tell me anything else about what happened? At the check up this afternoon, you said you didn't have any concerns."

"I didn't. This is out of nowhere." Missy's trembling hand caressed my ears. Poor girl. I hated doing this to her, though the attention was nice. "But look at him! He's ... he's all droopy!"

"Yeah, it's really strange." He clicked his tongue. "Look, I can take some blood samples, do some labs, keep him for observation overnight."

Bloodwork? Oh tail no! A cat has his limits. I leaped off the table and scurried to hide behind the trash bin in the corner. Realizing I'd blown my cover, I peeped out again. The humans gaped at me.

"Well, something woke him up." Doctor Spencer chuckled.

Missy's mouth opened and closed like a goldfish. Not a good look on a human—though I do like goldfish. Pretending I'd done nothing wrong, I started to wash my paws.

"Cap? Are you all right?" She started towards me. Her jacket pocket buzzed. Flinching, Missy fished out her phone, looked at the screen, and grimaced. "Dana wants her stupid pics. Dang it! What am I going to tell her? That I spent the last hour being hustled by a hypochondriac cat?" She shoved her phone back into her pocket, leaving the text unanswered.

"I don't think cats have the ability to fake illnesses." Doctor Spencer smiled.

I snorted. Fancy Vet-Man thought he knew all about cats, did he?

"Well, he certainly got me down here in a panic only to make a miraculous recovery." She let out a long breath, her shoulder slumping.

"Maybe he *did* eat something. You said he threw up? That could've gotten it out of his system, and we were viewing the after effects. It's hard to know. Wish he could tell us." The doctor got down on his knees and inched towards me. "I want to have one last look at him, and maybe even go through with those blood tests, just to be safe."

The thought of needles puffed my tail up. I bolted around the doctor and hid behind Missy's sneakers.

"Cap!" She wobbled. Her face went gray, and she gripped the edge of the exam table.

Doctor Spencer leaped to his feet. "Are you all right?"

"Yeah, fine, I … I need to sit …" She took a step towards a chair in the corner, stumbled, and toppled to the floor.

"Missy!" Doctor Spencer and I scrambled towards her. His foot hit my stomach. I yowled. He yelped, flailed madly, and landed hard on his rump. I barely slid out of his way in time to avoid being crushed.

Stupid, clumsy Vet-Man! Get out of the way and let me get to my human!

Paws slipping on the tiled floor, I managed to skid to a halt beside Missy's face. I nudged her, hoping she'd open her eyes. She moaned.

"Miss Novak? Missy?" The doctor crawled to our side. "Can you hear me?" He rolled her onto her back. "Darnit, I don't do people medicine ... okay, first aid training ... umm ... Feet above heart level?" He pulled her feet up into his lap. "Loosen restrictive clothing..."

He reached for her jacket's zipper. I hissed at him and swatted his hand away. What did he think he was going to do?

Missy groaned and opened her eyes. "What happened?"

"You passed out." The doctor touched her face. "Are you all right? I can call an ambulance."

"No, don't do that." She propped herself up on her elbows.

"Easy!" He put out his hand. "You don't want to stand too fast. Did you hit your head?"

"No. I'm fine."

He furrowed his brow. "People don't pass out when they're fine."

I hopped onto Missy's lap and bumped my head into her chin.

"Well, I'm starving, but otherwise fine." She flushed. "I didn't eat anything today. Kept meaning to, but things kept happening to get in the way. I really just need a snack."

"Of course!" He stood. "Don't try to stand while I'm gone, all right?"

"I guess." She grimaced.

He bolted from the exam room.

"Great, Missy. Toppling over because you were too stupid to remember to do something as basic as eat even one meal today. Awesome impression to make on a guy."

Her pocket buzzed again. Scooting to sit against the wall, she examined her phone. "Oh, give me a break, Dana."

Snuggling into Missy, I purred with all my might. Purring is good for humans. It's something all cats know, even if humans don't. My purring would keep Missy from falling down again.

Doctor Spencer hurried back, clutching a granola bar and a bottle of juice. "I got these from the vending machine." He sat beside her and took the top off the juice. "Here you go."

"Thanks." Missy sipped slowly. "I didn't mean to cause such a fuss. I was about to eat when Cap had his ... whatever it was. It scared me so much I didn't even think about not having eaten."

"Yeah, I get why that would be terrifying." The doctor scratched at the base of my spine. A shiver passed through my body. I had to hand it to the guy, he had a way with cats.

"Do you have any idea what caused it?" Missy whispered, as if concerned I could hear. I could, of course, but I'd never let on that I understood. No, a cat needed to keep that little secret.

He shrugged. "No idea. I mean, I'd like to schedule a follow up to do those tests I mentioned, but if it's all right with you, I'd prefer to get you home safe rather than worry about that tonight. Cap's important, yes, but you're more important, if you don't mind me saying so."

She dropped her gaze and focused on me. "He seems to be doing all right now, anyway."

"Yeah, like I said, if it was something he ate, he may have gotten it out of his system when he threw up." He stood. "You drove here?"

She nodded. "Yes."

He rubbed the back of his neck. "I'd really rather you not drive yourself home. Passing out at the wheel could be disastrous. Also, are you sure you didn't hit your head when you fell? You went down fast."

"I'm sure. I'm fine." She stood, knocking me off her lap. I gave a disgruntled meow.

"I'd feel so much better if you went to the emergency room, though." He offered her the chair, and she sat back down. I hopped into my rightful place on top of her. "I mean, do you live alone?"

"Just me and Cap, but I swear I'm all right."

"Is there a friend you can call? Someone who can drive you home and sit with you, just in case? Please, for my peace of mind?" His blue eyes widened in a sincere way that reminded me of a puppy's...except not horrific.

"I'm really ..." She stopped when their eyes met. A tremor ran through her body and into me. Quite disconcerting. My ears twitched. "I guess I can call my friend, Dana. She's been bugging me enough tonight that I know she isn't too busy."

"Good." He handed her the granola bar. "I can stay with you until she gets here. If that doesn't make you uncomfortable, of course. I wouldn't want to—"

"No, it's fine!" she said a little too quickly.

They stared at each other like a pair of awkward kittens whose eyes had just opened. I shook my head and licked my paw. Silly humans.

"I appreciate you being so concerned," she said.

Missy dialed Dana. The phone rang ... and rang and rang. "Voicemail," Missy said after a moment. "She was just texting me ... maybe it's on vibrate. I'll text her." She tapped on her phone for a minute. "There. Hopefully she'll see that and get back to me soon."

The clock on the exam room wall ticked quietly. I continued to wash myself and enjoy Missy's pets for a while, but after some time, even I was getting bored—and hungry. My thoughts turned to the tuna I'd left at the apartment and how unfortunate it was that I'd had to barf up what little I'd gotten down.

"I'm sorry," Missy finally said. "I'm sure you have somewhere better to be."

He laughed. "Not really. Honestly, I was going to finish up some paperwork and head home to a good book or maybe a movie."

"Sounds like my idea of a good time." She smiled. "What would you watch?"

"Actually, after your visit today and mentioning your cat was named after my favorite Avenger, I got the desire to watch *The Winter Soldier* again."

"Oh, that's one of my favorites." Missy's fingers squeezed into my fur, but I put up with it. She seemed to be having a good time. "You should see the fan art I did after I watched it!"

He arched his eyebrows. "You do fan art?"

"Yeah, I'm actually an artist ... well, an artist, designer, illustrator ... I kind of have to wear a lot of hats to make enough to live off of. I wish the starving artist thing was a myth, but I've at least advanced to 'always hungry but surviving' levels." She laughed. I snickered inwardly. I'd heard her practice that line to the bathroom mirror once or twice.

"Amazing. I don't suppose you have anything you can show me on you?"

"Well." She pulled up something on her phone and passed it to him. "That's my online shop. I sell prints and stickers and t-shirts."

He concentrated on the phone then raised his eyes to hers. "These are excellent. A lot of Cap themed stuff, I see."

I stuck my chest out. Of course.

"Yeah, he's kind of a big part of my life."

"I can tell. He seems like a big deal online. I didn't realize I would be taking on celebrity patients when I started here."

Missy and I both beamed at him ... me only for a second before I caught myself, shuddered, and returned my attention to paw washing. If Missy was going to get all nip-brained over this guy, it would be up to me to keep a cool head.

Nibbling on her granola bar, Missy fielded questions about her work and how she'd started her business.

"The ironic thing is I moved cross country after school to work at a start-up downtown—Dana's then-boyfriend-now-fiance's company, actually," she said. "It was her idea. They met at college, and she followed him here afterwards. It seemed like a good opportunity, but it was never really what I wanted to do." She glanced at her still silent phone and sighed. "When I finally got the gumption to try and make my little side business selling my own designs full-time, there wasn't enough money for another big move, even though all my family and long-term friends are back in Michigan. That's also why I embarrassingly don't have anyone but Dana to call right now even though she's taking forever." She typed into the phone, grunted, and shoved it into her pocket. A few seconds later it finally buzzed. She eyed the text, and her scowl deepened. "She says she won't be able to get away for another hour. Suggests I head home and she'll drop by on her way back from dinner to check in on me."

"You told her you fainted and really shouldn't be driving yourself right now, right?" Doctor Spencer frowned.

"I did, but from the typos in these texts, I'm kind of thinking she's on the tipsy side, so her driving me home wouldn't be much better." Scooping me up into her arms, Missy stood. "Look, I know you're a doctor so you probably are thinking worst case medical scenarios and getting sued and all, but I've already taken up enough of your evening. I promise, I'm fine. I simply need to get home and rest."

"I mean, I can't keep you here." He grimaced. "Still, maybe a compromise?" He hopped off the exam table where he'd been sitting. "Let me drive you home?"

She hesitated. "I can't ask you to do that. How will you get from my apartment to your place?"

He flashed her his phone. "I've got an app for that."

"I can't make you pay for a ride."

"No one is making me do anything." He held up his hand. "I'm offering because I'm a nice guy—or maybe because like you said, I'm a panicky medical professional who doesn't want to get sued for letting a woman who was under my care pass out in traffic and die in a horrible, fiery car crash."

She snorted. "You do remember that you are my *cat's* doctor, not *my* doctor?"

"Oh, trust me, I'm very aware of that." His lips curled into a mischievous grin. "So, let me drive you home? Please?"

Her fingers kneaded into my muscles. I could feel her heart beating against me as she clutched me to her chest. Normally I didn't like close, squeezy hugs, but some instinct told me now was the moment to be still.

"Okay," she said. "Can I buy you dinner at least?" She grinned. "I also have an app for that."

"You had me at 'dinner.'" He smirked.

Chapter Seven

After that, Missy unfortunately shoved me into my cage which was in turn deposited in the back seat. Resigned to my fate of a poor view, I tucked my paws beneath my chest and listened as they discovered many astonishing things like that she had his favorite band on her driving playlist and that they liked the same delivery pizza and could even agree on toppings. I guessed this might be what humans called 'chemistry' though to me it was a little gut churning. Eyes half closed, I endured the ride home in somber silence.

We reached the apartment building just as the pizza delivery man, summoned by Missy's app, pulled up. The doctor took my carrier so Missy could tip the pizza guy and didn't relinquish me as they made their way up the stairs. When we passed the second floor landing, raucous shouts rang out, and Missy winced.

The doctor gave a low whistle. "Sounds like someone's having a party."

"Yeah, I had an invite, but Cap's mystery illness got in the way—honestly, I should thank him." She tapped the outside of my carrier. "Extra cat treats for you, Capsicle."

My mouth watered. I hoped they were the salmon flavored ones.

Reaching the apartment door, she shifted the pizza box to one side and fumbled with the keys. Sensing something was amiss, I pressed my nose against the door.

"I've actually never had a man in my apartment." Her cheeks reddened. "I mean, I know this is all purely professional, but still, it's kind of a milestone for me."

"I'm glad I could be here to mark it." He set my cage down so he could take the pizza. "Look, about dinner—we only met today, and I get why you might not want me in your place. I do kind of want to be around in case you pass out again, but if your friend is going to be here soon, maybe I should just wait in the lobby?"

"No!" she protested. "You've been a complete gentleman, and it's not like we'll be alone for long. Dana should be here when her dinner's over. There's no reason you can't hang out until she arrives."

Once inside, I bounded from my cage as soon as Missy opened it and headed straight for the kitchenette. The tuna was still there, waiting. Room temperature, but still delectable. Missy cleaned up my vomit from earlier in the evening with a napkin and some disinfectant before bringing out the paper plates and a couple of cans of soda. I finished my tuna and settled on the couch a little ways from them to watch and clean my whiskers.

"Sorry you missed your party, but thank you for the pizza." The doctor raised his soda in a mock toast.

She snorted. "I wasn't really keen to go to Hunter's whatever-it-was game watching thing, anyway. An evening with my cat and someone who appreciates the fine art of the comic book flick is more my speed. Anyway, I owe you after I monopolized your evening, Doctor Spencer."

"I think we've reached the point where you can call me Evan." He chuckled. "You're actually the first real connection I've made since moving here."

"You're from out of state, too?" She sat up a little straighter.

"Well, not that dramatic. Out of town. I returned to my home town after vet school, but didn't find the opportunities I'd hoped, so when I saw the opening here, I applied." He took a bite of pizza then washed it down with a swig of soda. "It's close enough to home that I still drive to see my parents on holidays, but other than that, it's hard to justify the trip. For the last couple of months, it's been mostly me and Peg, all on our lonesome."

Missy's face fell, and I stiffened. Who was this Peg?

"Is Peg your girlfriend?"

"Of a sort." A sly smile crept across his lips. He pulled out his phone and flipped to a picture. "Agent Peggy Carter, my constant companion."

Visible relief swept over Missy's face. I climbed into her lap for a peek. On the phone was a picture of the sweetest little cat I'd seen in a long time: sleek black fur, bright amber eyes, and a flirtatious white moustache-patch beneath her precious little nose. My fur stood on end.

"She's lovely." Missy passed Evan the phone again.

Oh yes, she was lovely. She was purr-fect.

"Yeah, I'm aiming to break gender stereotypes and prove that it's not just crazy cat ladies out there. There are a couple of us crazy cat gents, too."

"Honestly, I wouldn't trust a man who didn't like cats." Missy bent down to brush her cheek against mine. "Shows they are gentle and responsible enough to take care of small things but secure enough to handle someone with an independent streak."

He tilted his head to one side. "That's very insightful."

"Also, now that I know your cat is named Agent Carter, I really feel that she and Cap have to meet someday." Missy scratched my ears.

"Obviously. That's fate." He smirked. "Let's just try to keep him away from arctic regions, all right?"

Missy roared with laughter.

Even more certain that I'd made the right choice bringing these two together, I decided it was time for a drastic step. I leaped from Missy's lap onto his. Evan recoiled then ran his hand gently down my spine.

Missy raised her eyebrows. "Cap! Should I feel betrayed?"

"Nah, he's just being friendly. I'm flattered, though." Evan's finger tickled my chin. "After all, he's my favorite Avenger."

"Mine too. Of course, the actor playing him doesn't hurt." Missy cleared her throat, dropped her gaze, and mumbled. "You, uh, kind of remind me of him, you know? In the eyes especially."

Evan froze mid-scratch. "That has to be the best compliment I've received in my life."

They sat in silence, Evan absentmindedly ruffling my fur—the wrong way, but I could put up with it—and Missy growing redder-faced by the second. She angled slightly towards him. His hand ceased petting me and wandered onto the couch cushion between them. Her hand crept towards his like an anxious mouse afraid of a trap but wanting the cheese. In response, my heart rate quickened. Was this going to happen?

Missy's phone rang. Fur on end, tail a bottle brush, I jumped two feet, and skidded behind the couch to hide. Stupid, loud, annoying, poorly-timed phone calls.

"Oh, it's Dana. Maybe she needs me to let her in the building."

I peered out as Missy answered the phone.

"What? ... It's really loud there ... yeah, I'm home now. Are you coming over soon?" Missy's brow furrowed. "I can't hear you very well. When did you say you'd be over?" Missy's mouth opened and closed several times. The thrumming techno music echoed through the phone to the extent that I could hear it several feet away. "Have you been drinking? ... Yes, but the whole point was to have someone here *tonight* not tomorrow ... Okay, nevermind. Just forget it." Missy hit the "end call" button before Dana could've had a chance to respond. I hopped up on the couch next to her again, my nose in the air, feeling somehow vindicated that awful Dana was being predictably awful. If Missy had just paid attention to how she treated me, we could've gotten rid of that human equivalent of a thermometer up the tail end years ago.

"She's not coming over?" Evan frowned.

"Said she can't get away from her social obligation—from her word-slurring and the music in the background, she means drunken clubbing." Missy sniffed and tossed the phone to the side. It landed softly on the cushion next to me. I batted it a few times, sending it onto the carpet. Missy didn't move to pick it up. "She suggested she could swing by tomorrow morning to check in on me. I told her not to bother."

Evan let out a long breath. "If you don't mind me saying so, you could use a better friend."

"One less wedding present to buy." Missy crossed her arms over her chest. "I wonder if I can still return that stupid dress."

"Yeah, well, considering you haven't complained of feeling woozy or dizzy, maybe you were right and I was panicking for nothing." He pushed a stray lock of blond hair away from his forehead. "You'll probably be all right alone tonight."

At a loss for what else to do to keep him here, I meowed, my gaze darting between them. Seriously? They weren't going to end it here, were they?

"Yeah, I'm fine. I told you, it was only because I didn't eat all day ... though the stress of Cap going all limp on me didn't help anything." She narrowed her eyes at me. "I wish I knew what was up with him. Maybe I should make a follow up appointment ... though I guess you don't have the ability to schedule me right now, huh?"

"No, you'll have to call the office for that." He stood. My heart sank. This was over? Should I vomit again? Fake another seizure? Trip him on the way out so he'd break a leg?

"Well, thank you for all you've done, for me and Cap." Missy rose from the couch. There was barely enough room for me between them, and I wisely chose not to insert myself into that space. "I've known you less than twelve hours, and you've already proven yourself a better friend than someone who has been in my life since college. You're ... kind of a super hero in my book."

"Dang." He blinked. "You know how to make a guy feel ..." He stopped. I leaned closer, only my superb balance preventing me from falling off the couch altogether. My tiny heart fluttered in my chest.

Please, Mr. Vet-Man. Please don't leave without giving my human some hope.

Evan closed his eyes. "Missy, this is a little sudden, but I kind of believe in fate, and fate is practically waving signal flags in my face right now." He eased nearer to her. His hand strayed to her shoulder. Missy shivered. "After Cap's check up today, all I could think of was you," Evan continued. "I kept telling myself it was ridiculous, but I went over every word we'd said to each other over and over again and ... and I don't do that. I'm not an obsessive guy. If anything, I'm a little too laid back, perfectly happy just to do my job then go home to my cat and a good movie. After you left the clinic, though ... I obsessed. I obsessed hard."

"You did?" Missy's voice quavered.

"Oh yeah." His fingers trailed down her arm before wrapping around her hand. "I know we just met, so this is an extremely low pressure offer. Still, I don't want to see you in the context of a follow-up exam for Cap—though yeah, make that call. I really want to know what's up with him. I want to see you, well, as a date, maybe to a good comic book movie?"

"I'd really like that," she stammered. Her hold on his hand tightened.

"Is tomorrow too soon?" His head lowered towards hers. A purr rumbled to life in my chest. I couldn't look away.

"Not too soon at all." She reached for his face, her fingers trailing from his ear down to his chin. Then, as if his lips were the elusive red dot, she lunged for him. He met her half way, his arm circling her waist, his mouth pressing against hers.

If cats could dance, I would've been dancing. I'd done it! I'd gotten my human her own human! Words could not express how brilliant I was!

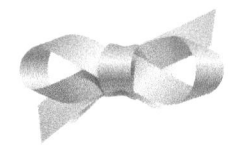

Chapter Seven

It's been a while since my human ran smack into Peggy's human's lips ... Peggy is my girlfriend now. She's the most precious puss I've ever met. I like to call her Black Magic. We spend a lot of time grooming each other, and she's even convinced me to share my favorite toys. Also, with two humans supervising our care, the treats are double.

We did have to spend a little bit of time with Evan's little sister during the honeymoon last month, but as cat-sitters go, she was a pretty good sort. Peggy and I took turns on her lap, and we found out that we could convince her our feedings were three times a day, not two, if we meowed enough.

Evan and Missy are sickeningly adorable together. Missy's started a new line of couple themed illustrations to commemorate their courtship, featuring pictures of me and Peggy cuddling, mostly. I guess it's selling well. At least she's always printing out new shipping labels.

Evan is still a little suspicious about whatever ailment had me in his office that fateful night, but some things must remain a mystery.

After all, humans aren't entitled to all of our feline secrets.

Still, as humans go, Missy and Evan are first rate. I'm definitely going to keep them—and Peggy—forever.

The End

Whisker Width

On the eve of her thirtieth birthday, Kara decided to bite the bullet and get a cat.

Kara had always liked cats but hadn't owned one since her senior cat, Einstein, passed away at the ripe old age of sixteen. She'd thought about replacing him, even window-shopped a few shelters, but her friends already snickered at her cat-themed socks and her love for all things "kitten." As far as they were concerned, if she got a cat before she got a boyfriend, she might as well apply for her "crazy cat lady" license while she was at it.

So instead, Kara had accompanied them to speed dating, and noisy clubs, and singles mixers, and other forms of torture where no one appreciated her clever feline-related puns. It wasn't that she didn't like people. The right sort of people were awesome; the wrong sort, the sort that wanted to talk sports or politics rather than get into a "Princess Bride" quote-off... Honestly, Kara would just rather hang out with cats.

Friday night was the final straw. Her coworkers had set her up with a blind date who, after about ten minutes of awkward conversation, just gave up and spent the rest of dinner texting. Rude, but she was used to that from humans by now. It was when he set his phone down to pick up his beer and she got a glimpse of his latest text exchange that she'd finally had enough.

DB: How's the date, bro?
M: Meh.
DB: That bad, huh?
M: She's cute but way too fluffy.

Fluffy? And he said it like that was a bad thing? Kara walked out of the date halfway through the meal. Well, she'd got a doggy bag. She wasn't an idiot.

But delicious leftovers aside, she was through with the dating game. She couldn't believe she'd put on contacts and makeup for that jerk.

Who needed men anyway? Who needed people at all? Kara was going to get herself a cat!

So that was why, as soon as her shift was up on Monday, she slipped off to the local animal shelter to meet her new best friend.

Helping Paws Animal Rescue was located in a cold, industrial building that smelled strongly of wood shavings and wet dog. Well, Kara wasn't there for a dog. She knew what she wanted. She pulled open the heavy metal door, pushed her glasses further up her nose, and stared unashamedly into the eyes of the middle-aged volunteer. "I'm here to see your cats."

The husky, gray-haired woman nodded, slowly rose from her office chair, and unhooked a set of keys from the wall.

"Lou," she shouted. "You got the front?"

"Sure, Chris," a muffled voice came from the back office.

Not waiting for Lou, Chris nodded towards another heavy metal door, this one with a fogged glass window. The constant whines and yelps of what had to be a dozen puppies rose from beyond it, tearing at Kara's heartstrings. Well, she didn't have space for a dog, just a cat. Maybe cats weren't as boisterously desperate, but they needed love too.

They walked through a narrow corridor with metal cages on both sides—Kara doing her best to avoid the literal puppy-dog eyes coming at her from all directions—before opening a second door into a quiet room with a Plexiglas divider in the middle. On the other side of the divider rose a forest of carpeted cat trees.

"We had an adoption drive this weekend. Nine lives for nine dollars. Reduced our usual fee for cat adoption from $75 to just $9. Every cat fancier in the county, and some from as far as Portland, swarmed us, so I'm afraid we've only got a few cats left. No kittens." Chris narrowed her eyes, as if testing Kara's resolve with this announcement.

"An adult cat is fine." Kara resisted pressing her nose against the Plexiglas. A bundle of black fur spilled over the sides of one cat bed, and a tabby licked at a water bowl in the center of the room. Not much to choose from. She'd know the "one" when she met him, though, right?

Chris took a binder from a shelf. "These are the stats of our current residents. Do you know what sort of a companion—"

Something buzzed overhead, making Kara jump, then a voice echoed from an intercom speaker. "Chris, we've got a drop-off."

Chris mumbled under her breath. "Sorry, miss, but Lou doesn't have access to the main computer. I need to process the new arrival." She passed Kara the binder. "Why don't you read up on our current guests?"

With that she rushed out of the room, shutting the door behind her and leaving Kara separated from furry goodness by a thick layer of Plexiglas. Kara sighed and opened the folder. The first several pages had appealing pictures of kitties, but all stamped with "adopted." Even if they hadn't been, the paper just listed stats: age, health, whether they'd been turned in or rescued. She wasn't looking for statistics. She was looking for chemistry.

She sank into a nearby folding chair and rubbed her forehead. A prickling sensation rushed through her, like the bite of static electricity, and a haunting scent of cinnamon and ozone filled her nose. Something warm and soft brushed up against her legs. She leaped from her chair with a yelp.

A massive orange tabby cat blinked up at her. She blinked back. The cat rubbed against her ankles then flicked its tail and sat down to wash its paws.

Kara glanced at the Plexiglas. "How'd you get out?" Dropping to her haunches, she stroked the feline's spine. Energy prickled through her fingers. That explained the static. This cat was charged.

A rumbling purr rose from the animal. It gazed up at her with soulful amber eyes. Something about its face said "boy cat."

"Well, aren't you a handsome ginger gentleman," she cooed.

The cat gave an approving "mew" and continued to circle her, his tail tickling her nose. Something within her eased, and before she knew what was happening, she was sitting cross-legged on the cold linoleum floor with a heavy bundle of cat in her lap and purrs vibrating through her entire being. She couldn't remember the last time she'd been so happy.

The scent of cinnamon intensified. Perhaps the shelter had one of those time-release wall plug-ins. They probably needed it to combat all the various animal odors. Closing her eyes, she focused on the hum of the cat and the scent of the cinnamon. A vision came unbidden: one of grassy fields and stone towers. Something from a movie? A book she'd read? Maybe. It was a nice daydream, no matter what had caused it. Every muscle in her body softened, and she slumped against the wall, mechanically stroking the cat's silky fur.

A figure crossed the space before her, tall and willowy. With a deep voice, he called out, "Caius? Caius? Where'd you get to?"

Now that seemed an odd detail to dream up. And come to think of it, she'd never really had daydreams this photo-realistic before. On a whim, she opened her mouth to respond to the dream-man.

"Where did you get a cat? They're all locked up." Chris's question snapped Kara back into the present. The cat meowed in annoyance and hopped from Kara's lap.

Embarrassed at being caught sitting on the floor, Kara stood. "He just showed up. I like him though. Is he up for adoption?"

Chris hoisted the cat off the ground. He yowled and wriggled for freedom.

"Huh. I have no idea where this cat came from. He wasn't here this morning." Chris stuffed the cat beneath one arm like a bag of kitty litter and left the room. Kara scrambled after her, through the gauntlet of desperate dogs, back to the tiny front office. An elderly man in a trucker hat and flannel leaned back in the office chair, scrolling down his smartphone screen.

"Lou, you know you're not supposed to take in new animals without registering them. This one wasn't even in a cage, just wandering around loose." Chris pulled a cat carrier out from under the desk. The cat meowed and splayed his legs, but eventually lost his fight and went into the carrier.

Lou blinked. "I didn't take in any cats this morning." He squinted into the cage. "That's a big orange boy. I'd remember him. Nope. I haven't seen him before. Did he maybe come in last night?"

"No, I locked up last night. We didn't get any new cats yesterday. Just that pit bull and the pair of ferrets."

"Well, he couldn't have gotten in here on his own." The two volunteers continued to discuss the appearance of the strange cat as if Kara wasn't even in the room.

The cat stared through the air holes in the top of the carrier, directly into Kara's heart. Yes, chemistry. She and this cat had chemistry.

She cleared her throat. "Excuse me, but I think that cat is the one I want."

Lou and Chris paused and stared at her.

Kara stepped closer to the cat carrier. Goosebumps popped out over her arms. Yes, she really *was* a crazy cat lady, and she wasn't afraid to admit it. "Can I take him home?"

"I'm afraid it's not that easy," Chris said. "We have procedures. He needs to see a vet, get entered into the system." She opened a file cabinet, her shoulder blocking Kara's view of the cage. Desperation flooded Kara's chest.

"I'll see to his vet bills. I'd just like to…reserve him, to be sure no one else takes him, you know."

"We don't really put holds on our cats. They aren't hotel rooms." Chris sniffed. "What if the vet visit finds a microchip? He'll have to go back to his real family then. Even if he's not chipped, his real family could be looking for him. Wouldn't be responsible for us to promise him to someone before we've held him a while to see if he's claimed."

Stomach tightening, Kara had to admit this made sense. "Oh. Yeah. How long will that take?"

"A week, maybe, depending on what we find in the vet exam." Lou pointed to a wall where a series of printouts advertised the various pets waiting for adoption. "You didn't get a chance to meet the others, though. Maybe one of them will catch your eye."

"No, I think I'll wait." Kara sighed. "I'll keep an eye on the website for him."

With one last longing look at the cat carrier, she turned and left the shelter.

.. ⚓ ..

ON HER WAY TO HER SECOND-story apartment, Kara passed the super, Mr. Elliott.

"Hey, Mr. E." She gave him what she hoped was a convincing smile. Mr. E knew the business of all the tenants, including her recent disaster of a first date. The elderly man had been sweetly concerned, but she wasn't in the mood for sympathy right now. No, she just wanted to get in and see if the shelter had updated their "up for adoption" page yet.

"Ah, Kara." Mr. E smiled. "Home a little late tonight. Hot date?" He winked.

"Just with a bottle of wine and a TV marathon." She laughed. "Going to rewatch that episode where the detective has to solve a murder with the victim's cat as the only witness, I think."

"Oh, that's a good one. I might have to rewatch that too. Have a good night."

Unlocking her apartment door, Kara breathed a long sigh. She should've known in the days of modern bureaucracy it wouldn't be as simple as showing up and picking out a cat. For all she knew, cats had to be holistically matched with the ideal owners. No, not owners. That wasn't politically correct. "Human life partners." There, that sounded better. Still, she felt a little foolish for the bag of litter and box of canned food she'd purchased...and the impulse buy of a cat bed and ten-pack of toys that would be arriving via Amazon in the morning...and the "going to meet my new best friend now" tweet she'd sent...

Oh, goodness gracious, she was a mess.

"Maybe there is something wrong with me," Kara whispered, her hand still clenched around the doorknob, her mind unwilling to open it to reveal the cold, empty studio apartment inside with only the cold comforts of a laptop and a half-bottle of zinfandel to welcome her.

No, she couldn't be like that. One bad date and a setback in the cat department wouldn't ruin her day.

She'd get her cat.

Soon.

Maybe the shelter had updated the site already!

She opened the door.

A pair of glowing eyes stared at her from the couch.

Kara shrieked.

Stumbling back into the hallway, she slammed the door shut. Wait. From the size and placement of those eyes, it wasn't a big creature. Not a monster. A rat? A possum? Not great, but not life-threatening. She glanced down the hall. No sign of Mr. E, but it would be good to know what she was dealing with before she called him up. Let him know what size of traps to bring.

Heart pounding, Kara eased the door open while her other hand fumbled for the light switch.

A large orange tabby hopped from her couch and crossed to her. He sat at her feet and gazed up at her with those wise amber eyes.

A cat.

And not just any cat. *The* cat.

She swallowed. But it couldn't be. Even if the cat had managed to escape the shelter, how had it found her apartment and got there before she could? No, this was a really weird coincidence. This had to be a different cat.

"Meow, purr." The cat circled her ankles, throat rumbling like a distant thunderstorm. Tingles shot through her, accompanied by the scent of cinnamon. As ridiculous as it was, she knew, this was the same cat.

This was *her* cat. She gathered him up and squeezed him to her face. "It's all right, Caius," for somehow she was certain that was his name. "You're home. You're home."

. . ⁓ . .

A MORE LAW-ABIDING part of Kara's brain wondered if she should call the shelter and let them know she had their cat, but a firm feeling that Caius wasn't *their* cat but *her* cat had implanted itself deep in her soul. As unreasonable as that feeling might be, Kara couldn't risk them taking Caius away from her. Not when he'd come so far to be with her. They had chemistry. All her life, she'd accepted that magic wasn't real, that it was only in her books and movies. Now, however, she knew the truth: magic existed in the form of cats. It was a subtle, everyday sort of magic, of course, but she'd take what she could get.

Kara fell asleep with Caius's claws kneading into her shoulders. It hurt a little, but she didn't mind it. His purrs soothed her soul. In her dreams, she and her new kitty sunbathed in green fields accompanied by the scent of cinnamon and a deep masculine voice calling out, "Caius! Caius!"

Finally her eyes drifted open. Caius rubbed against her face.

"Good morning, dear." She ruffled his stately ears. Rolling over to look for her glasses on the nightstand, she paused. Something glittered beside the paperback of *How to Catch a Unicorn* she'd been reading. She squinted and leaned closer. The object came into focus as a silver flower with frosted leaves and petals. Some sort of Christmas decoration? Where had that come from?

Reaching for her glasses for a better look, her hand brushed the flower, and it crumbled into dust.

What the heck?

Bolting upright, she slammed her glasses onto her face. Nothing. Nothing was there.

Well, she hadn't been wearing her glasses. It was possible she'd just imagined a flower. What was that thing where a person saw faces in appliances? Yeah, that thing. That thing had made her imagine a sparkly flower in the dust.

"I need coffee."

What with seeing things, Kara didn't want to wait for a pot to brew for her caffeine infusion, so she cracked open one of her emergency cans of Liquid Sanity iced coffee. With that chugged, she and Caius settled in for a nice breakfast of eggs and Pawsome brand Chicken and Liver Pate. Caius cleaned his plate then daintily cleaned his paws.

She glanced at her phone. "I'm sorry, boy, but I have to go now. Will you be all right for a few hours on your own? I work right down the street, so I can come back and check on you at lunch, all right?"

Caius paused in his grooming, ears twitching. She patted his head. "I'll leave the TV on, all right? I've got all the best episodes of that fake psychic show recorded. You'll love it."

Caius yawned and settled into a perfect "cat loaf," his tail and paws tucked neatly beneath his body. Kara sighed. He was so, so adorable.

The morning at work crawled along. Between filling customer orders, she closed her eyes and thought about how she finally had someone waiting at home for her. If she allowed her mind to drift, she could smell the cinnamon and hear the voice from her dreams chanting Caius's name. The voice tasted vaguely of cinnamon, which was an odd thing to think, but somehow it felt right.

When lunchtime arrived, she clocked out and zipped to her car. The ten-minute drive to her apartment building might as well have been an hour. What if Caius thought she'd abandoned him? Did cats understand about day jobs? She barreled down the hall, jammed her key into the lock, and yanked the door open.

"I'm home!" she shouted.

Nothing.

Swallowing, she eased the door shut behind her. Well, cats slept a lot. He'd probably found a place to curl up for a nap. She'd make them both something to eat. That would draw him out. She put a Nutritious Options meal in the microwave and pulled back the tab on another can of Pawsome Chicken and Liver Pate.

"Caius?" she called. "I have num nums!"

No answer.

She bit her bottom lip. "Dinner's served, your meow-jesty." She laughed nervously at her own pun. Caius didn't emerge.

Kara panicked. She tore about the apartment, looking under the couch, the bed, in the closet, the bathtub, even checking the various cabinets she doubted he could open on his own. No sign of her cat. Her lunch hour was flitting away, and Caius was nowhere to be seen.

But how? How could he have gotten out? The door was shut. The windows were shut. He couldn't have walked through the walls.

"Caius, where are you?" What if he had gotten out? He'd somehow made it to her home from the shelter, so obviously he could escape buildings. The traffic on her street moved so fast. What if something happened to him?

Grabbing her keys and her phone, she rushed from the apartment and ran smack into Mr. E.

"Whoa there!" He held up his hands, one hand holding a half-empty carton of lightbulbs.

A thought struck her. Mr. E sometimes entered the apartments to fix things. He had a key. While normally he told her if he'd be stopping by for repairs, even while she was out, if something was urgent, he might go ahead and enter. Right? What if he had and Caius had slipped out?

"Have you seen my cat?" she gasped.

He raised his eyebrows. "No. I didn't even know you had a cat. Did you get it recently?"

Forcing herself to draw deep breaths, she fumbled for an explanation as to how Caius had come into her life. He'd just appeared. That wasn't normal, that wasn't natural, but why would anyone expect normal or natural from an extraordinary cat like Caius?

"Yes, I just got him." She opened the door to her apartment. The can of cat food sat untouched on the table. Orange fur coated a section of the fleece throw draped across her couch, so he *had* been there. She wasn't going crazy. She did have a cat.

Mr. E poked around the apartment. "You know, cats can slip through just about anything and wedge themselves in the tightest spots. They have those whiskers for a reason. If their whiskers can fit, the rest of them can too. They're like kitty parking guides." He chuckled.

"I checked the whole apartment though. Twice." She crossed her arms. Caius wasn't just tucked away in some corner. He was missing. She could feel that he wasn't there. Something absent from the air, a thinness she couldn't explain, but which meant no Caius. Still, even as she thought it, she knew how crazy that would sound, and she kept quiet. She couldn't expect Mr. E to understand the magical mystery that was Caius.

"Well, if he did slip out, he wouldn't have gone far. Grab a can of food, and we'll look out by the dumpsters."

Kara and Mr. E circled the building, calling for Caius, but no one came out. Finally they stopped in the parking lot. She set the can of cat food on her car's hood and wiped the gravy from her hand onto her jacket.

"I can help you get the word out, at least." Mr. E smiled sympathetically. "What does this boy of yours look like?"

"Big orange tabby." *Piercing soulful amber eyes, electric energy, deep throaty purr...*

"Huh." Mr. E gazed towards the apartment building. He tilted his head to one side, squinted, then pointed. "You mean like that."

Kara followed his finger to a second-story window. *Her second-story window* if she wasn't mistaken. Sitting, staring out at them, was Caius. She squeaked, "Thank you!" and took off at a run.

Bursting into the apartment, she fell to her knees as Caius hopped down from the windowsill and strolled towards her.

"Where were you? You made me look like an idiot out there. Why didn't you come when I called?"

His tail flicked against her nose. She patted him then glanced at the clock. Even if she left immediately, she'd be late for work. Well, she had a few sick days left, and one could argue there was definitely something wrong with her, getting so overwrought over a cat. "Let me call in, and then we can make some popcorn. Do you like cheese? I think I have some cheese."

. . ⚜ . .

THANKFULLY, KARA'S boss accepted that her lunch wasn't agreeing with her without question. Soon Kara and Caius settled down on the couch with the laptop beside them. Caius accepted his backrubs, his gentle purr soothing Kara into a daze. Not feeling like anything challenging, she opened her browser to a "strangely satisfying" video playlist and watched contentedly as hot knives sliced through various substances.

After a bit, Caius stretched out to his full length, yawned, and hopped down from the couch.

"Litter box break?" She smiled. "Yeah, I could use one of those myself."

She headed for the bathroom. Before she could close the door behind her (a habit from growing up with three older brothers), a buzzing noise rose from the room she'd just left. Had her laptop playlist switched to some weird ambient track? She stuck her head out to check.

A bright flash blinded her, and she fell back into the wall, dazzled. Dots flitted about her vision, and the scent of cinnamon burned her nose.

"What was that?" Blinking several times, she cleared her vision. The room looked normal. Nothing out of place. She tiptoed into the middle of the room and paused the video on her laptop. A thought struck her. "Caius?" she called.

He was gone.

Kara sucked in air. *Don't panic. He's just in the kitchen.* She hurried to check, but there was no sign of the cat. *Under the bed?*

She got down on her hands and knees and pulled up the comforter. Nothing. Just dust. A lot of dust. Her eyes watered, and her nose itched. She sat up sneezing.

Flash!

She screamed and toppled to the ground.

"Meow?" Caius poked his head over the side of the bed and peered at her.

"How did you get there?" she snapped.

He hopped down. Two golden points of light whizzed over his head. They zipped around in circles, whistling and screaming...screaming? What sort of light screamed?

Trembling head to toe, Kara stumbled to her feet. The points of light sped towards her, their tone now obviously laughing. One collided with her cheek, burning like a spark from a firecracker. She slapped at it, but it wheeled away, snickering.

Caius hissed and sprang into the air. He thwacked the glowing...*thing* with his paw. It whimpered and hit the ground. The second dot of light zoomed over and pulled the first back into the air, chattering angrily. Caius yawned and flicked his tail. Another burst of light, and the mean light-thingies were gone.

Breath coming in ragged gasps, Kara gaped at Caius. "How did you do that?"

The cat scratched at his ears and disappeared in another flash.

. . ⚜ . .

KARA SPENT THE REST of the afternoon huddled on the couch while Caius exploded in and out of her apartment. If she didn't look directly at the blaze of light, she could kind of get the sense of it, like a peephole opening up to reveal the brilliance of the sun. Usually Caius casually slipped through these doorways on his own, but occasionally he brought "guests" with him. A few more of the light-thingies made it through. Kara armed herself with a fly swatter and chased them around the apartment until a second flash allowed them to escape back to wherever they came from.

One time, a part-deer-part-butterfly thing flitted through with iridescent wings and spindly azure legs. The puppy-sized creature frolicked for a bit before tripping over her coffee table and lying with a bewildered look in its big pink eyes, its wings fluttering madly. She'd almost gotten up enough courage to pet the adorably awkward thing when Caius pranced up to it. With a burst of light, both of them were gone.

As the shadows lengthened across her living area, Caius's portals—for what else could she call them?—came further and further between. Finally he curled up beside her, purring contentedly. She hesitantly stroked him.

So that explained how he had managed to make it from the shelter to her home, and maybe how he'd just shown up inside the shelter without any paperwork. Why was a magical, portal-summoning cat following her around, though?

"Why me?" she whispered.

He opened a single amber eye and sniffed.

"Yeah, I guess asking a cat, let alone a magic cat, for explanations is kind of stupid." She adjusted her glasses. "Well, at least I don't have to worry about you getting lost. Not really. You can just appear wherever you want to be, can't you?"

He playfully batted at her hand.

"And so far you haven't brought anything dangerous with you from...from wherever you go." She closed her eyes and remembered the visions of the green fields and the stone towers and the strange man. "I kind of wish you'd take me with you. If it has light...pixies? I think I'll call them pixies, then maybe it has other things I'd like to see. Like unicorns or elves or dragons. Actually, dragons might eat me. Huh." She weighed the positives of seeing elves and fairies against the potential negatives of being a dragon's lunch. Well, it wasn't as if her own world didn't have its dangers. "I guess I don't mind having a magic cat. Though try not to be obvious about it. Don't want the neighbors talking or some weird men in black showing up to recruit you for the Justice League or something." She snorted. "That movie would've been a *lot* more interesting with a teleporting cat."

Caius flicked his tail in obvious agreement.

A pinpoint of light swelled in the middle of the kitchen, but unlike Caius's usual portals, this one didn't burst in and out in a split second of brilliance. Rather it stayed steady, growing from a peephole to a porthole to a wall of radiant light that blocked her view of the refrigerator. She covered her eyes.

"Dangit, Caius. What are you up to now?"

Caius's ears pricked up. Meowing, he hopped off the couch and ran for the portal.

The light blinked out, but this time, Caius hadn't gone anywhere.

And he wasn't alone.

"Eep!" Kara grabbed the only weapon she had on hand—the fly swatter from her fight with the light-pixies—and brandished it in the direction of the tall, lean shadow in her kitchen.

"There you are!" a deep but melodious voice said.

Her eyes adjusted. A willowy man in a silver tunic and leggings leaned down to pat Caius's ears. The cat purred and rubbed against his legs. The strange man had long, flaxen hair, eerily lavender eyes, and pointed ears. He scooped up Caius. "You had me so worried. What were you thinking, staying away for so long?"

There was something decidedly unthreatening in the way he interacted with Caius. She set the flyswatter down and cleared her throat.

"Excuse me, but who are you and how did you get in my house?"

He started. His gaze swept up and down her. Kara shifted from foot to foot, suddenly aware of her pajama bottoms and messy ponytail.

"I'm sorry to intrude, my lady. I am Altair, Lord of the Fields of Light and the Seven Towers of Felancia." He bowed at the waist. "Unfortunately, my companion, Caius, has taken to disappearing of late. Cats are able to slip through the smallest gaps between the mortal and magical realms, so keeping him contained is near impossible. However, he rarely stays away as long as he has this time. Something here must be attracting him."

As if in response, Caius mewed and wriggled out of the stranger's arms. With a rumbling purr, he curled up on top of Kara's fuzzy unicorn slippers.

Altair's eyes widened. "Oh. Oh dear." He cleared his throat. "This is awkward, but apparently my cat has bonded to you."

"He seems to like me. I like him too."

Kara bent down and stroked Caius's chin. The cat shut his eyes, a look of pure contentment on his ginger face.

Yes, Caius belonged to Altair—though could a cat truly be said to belong to anyone? However, he *wanted* to be with Kara, and from the looks of things, Altair couldn't *stop* him from being with Kara. Still, even if the victory was hers, she could be gracious about it. Nothing good could come out of ticking off a gorgeous Elf-Prince, after all. She'd never realized lavender eyes could be so alluring. "I'm fine if he continues to visit. Do you need to take him back now?"

"Well, that's also a little awkward." He scratched his chin. "You see, while Caius can slip through cracks between the worlds as long as they are as wide as his whiskers, I, as an elflord, need a slightly wider opening to make it through. It took all my magic to open a portal large enough to follow him here, and I'm sorry to admit, I'm quite spent. I don't think I'll be able to manage another spell like that for a few more hours." His shoulders slumped.

"Oh!" Kara realized that his cheeks, which she'd just assumed were naturally pale, had a grayish pallor. She motioned to her couch. "Do you want some water?"

He sank onto the couch beside her laptop. "Yes, please. Though if you happen to have some wine, it would be good for my weary spirits."

"Certainly!" Suddenly glad she hadn't consumed her half-bottle of zinfandel, Kara set Caius down on Altair's lap and rushed for the kitchen. Look at her! About to be sipping wine with a handsome elflord. What sort of crazy cat lady would do that? The best sort, of course.

She poured two glasses. As she handed Altair his wine, he brushed a finger across the touchpad of her laptop, stirring to life the paused playlist. This video was a kinetic sand molding compilation. She flushed.

"Interesting." Altair tilted his head. "I had heard of these viewing boxes you mortals are so attached to, but I was under the impression they were for the distribution of information and entertainment. Not...this."

"Um, well, they do information and entertainment too." She sat beside him. The scent of cinnamon wafted from him. "I can switch it to something else, if you'd like. Or turn it off."

"No, this is fine." He stared intently as the silent pair of hands in the video smoothed the kinetic sand into a pleasingly symmetrical shape. "It is...oddly satisfying, in fact. Do you spend many evenings like this?"

Her cheeks warmed. "Not every evening. But some."

"Interesting. Perhaps I shall have to join Caius on his visits more often. Someday I can return the favor and host you in my golden halls. We have musicians and honey cakes. No viewing boxes, but I might be able to find other forms of entertainment to your liking."

"That sounds wonderful," she squeaked.

Altair and Kara sat in silence with Caius's front half on his lap and back half on hers, sipping red wine and watching satisfying videos. As first dates went, it was definitely in Kara's top five.

The End

The Unfinished Business of Mystie Whiskers

・・⚜・・

HUMANS SAY CATS HAVE nine lives, but this is not strictly true. I should know. My name is Mystie, and I'm a dead cat.

I wasn't always this way, of course. Once I was a charming, living, breathing, purring feline with a happy home and a loving human. I used to have mist gray fur—which was where I got my name. As a ghost my fur, all of me really, was more like real mist. No one suspected I was still there. Watching out for my human.

You might ask why I lingered. Why I didn't move on to take my rest—goodness knows I love a good nap. Well, to explain that, I have to tell you about my human.

Ryan wasn't my first human. Before Ryan there was a family who got me as a kitten but for reasons I'll never understand left me at a shelter after three or four summers. I heard words like "new apartment" and "baby," but no words like, "Sorry," or "We'll come back for you later." People are dumb sometimes. Anyway, after waiting around the shelter for a few weeks, I got over them. Especially when Ryan showed up.

I liked Ryan right away, and the feeling was obviously mutual because he adopted me and brought me back to his home. He took me with him when he saved up enough to buy his first house—our first house.

Ryan and I had a good life. He spent most nights reading books or playing video games with me in his lap. When he went to work, he'd leave the TV on for me to a screensaver with fish on it. I knew they weren't real fish—well, on an intellectual level at least. On an emotional, instinctive level, I sometimes couldn't resist scampering after them and batting at the screen. Ryan thought this was hilarious, which meant I tried not to do it when he got home and could watch. A lady cat has to have some dignity, after all.

We spent a lot of good years together, me and my human. A lot of chasing the red dot. A lot of ear scratches and chin rubs. Treats, naps, fish screensavers ... but all good things must come to the end.

The way this particular good thing ended was with a visit from an angel.

I hadn't been feeling too well that fateful night ... or for several nights before that, if I were honest. I put on a brave face about it because I didn't want Ryan getting any ideas about "vet visits" or anything nasty like that, but I felt tired, achy, and cold. The cold was the worst. There's nothing I love more than heat ... well, Ryan, I guess ... and catnip ... and those little fish-shaped treats that are crunchy on the outside and oozy in the middle—but I digress.

After tossing and turning at the foot of Ryan's bed for what felt like hours, I'd moved into the kitchen to sleep over the heater vent—my second favorite place to nap. The warmth seeped through my fur and into my bones and soon I was dreaming of fish-shaped cat treats that came alive and let me chase them through a sea of warm, dry water. If you don't know what dry water is, that's not my fault. Cats understand these things, but they are tiresome to explain to humans. Some time in the early morning I awoke with a start to find the angel standing over me.

I knew she was an angel right away, but I don't know if a human would've made the connection. She stood in the middle of the kitchen, wearing house slippers and a sweatshirt with a cartoon cat on it, a ball of yarn in one hand, a catnip mouse in another.

My ears flattened. It would've been odd enough, a strange human, even an elderly, harmless looking one, standing in our kitchen at three in the morning, but this human had an eerie glow, like she was standing in front of a light bulb.

She held out the catnip mouse, as if that would entice me. "Come, my good and faithful feline. You have served your human well for many years. It is time."

Alarmed, I skittered back a step—leaving my body behind. It lay there—the furry, fleshy, familiar bits of me—as if I were simply taking a nap, but somehow I was looking at me from the outside.

I glared at the angel. "Put me back!"

"Now, Mystie," the angel wagged a finger at me, further proving her angel-ness by understanding my words. "This happens to all cats, all life really, eventually. There's no reason to be skittish about it."

"Put a mouse in it, Grandma!" I hissed. "I can't leave my human now. He needs me."

She knelt down to face me. "My dear furry friend, all cats think their humans need them, and to some extent, maybe they do, but that still doesn't mean you can skip over your time."

I gazed desperately out the kitchen door towards Ryan's bedroom. I knew he'd be in there, alone. It was my job to keep his bed warm, to poke my cold nose against his face to wake him in the morning, to escort him to my food bowl and keep him company before and after work.

"But Ryan will be all alone without me."

The angel ruffled my ears. "Yes, my dear puss, he will be alone for a while. You will always have a special place in his heart, but soon he will find another cat. That is the way of things. Humans live through the lifetimes of many pets."

"But how will I know that pet will be good enough for him?" I whimpered. I'd had experience with more than one set of humans, so I knew Ryan was the special kind. The kind that kept a cat even when the cat vomited on his carpet or scratched at his furniture or meowed at inconvenient times. The kind who didn't leave a cat at a shelter, alone and confused, just because of words like "move" and "new baby." A human like Ryan didn't deserve to be alone.

I puffed up my fur and arched my back. "I'm not going."

"But Mystie ..." She ran her hand down my back.

I jerked away, hissing. "Not. Going."

The angel's brow furrowed, then she groaned, her hand dropping to her side again. "Seriously. This is the fourth time this week. Why couldn't I have been assigned canine duty? Or goldfish?"

Ignoring her whining, I daintily cleaned my paws and waited for her to go away.

"Look," the angel finally said. "I can't put you back in your body. That's not in my power, but what I can do is let you hang around for a bit, so you can see that your human is doing fine without you. If that's what it will take for you to move along peacefully, I'll come back and check on you again in a month, all right?"

I narrowed my eyes at her before giving a curt nod. After all, I could always refuse her again in another month. If this angel thought she was more stubborn than I was, she was sorely mistaken.

I blinked, and in the time it took my eyes to flutter back open, the angel was gone. Not feeling a need to sleep, I prowled the house for a while. I examined the photos on the book shelf. Pictures of me and Ryan. Ryan with his brother Carl at Carl's wedding. A fine picture of me wearing a brand new collar in front of our little fiber optic Christmas tree the previous year. We'd had a good run, me and Ryan. However, while I wasn't afraid of passing on, I just couldn't imagine the poor guy getting along without me.

Other than some long term gaming buddies, his brother, and his parents, Ryan really didn't have anyone. He worked during the day at his family's appliance repair shop and came home to me at night. That was his life, and while I was there, it had been enough. Without me, though? I couldn't see how that would be good for him. How he wouldn't get lonely or feel lost without me to take care of him.

I observed the sunrise through the back windows of our tiny two bedroom house. We had a small, fenced in yard which he didn't usually let me play in for fear I'd jump the fence and get hit by a car. Our living room had a nice view of it, though, and I watched as the stars faded and the sun rose. Birds hopped through the yard, plucking worms and insects out of the damp grass.

A shrill beeping echoed down the hall. Ryan's alarm. He'd be up soon. I slunk into the kitchen and stood near my now cold body to wait.

Ryan wandered into the room a little later, already wearing his coveralls for work. He opened the cabinet where my food was kept and clicked his tongue.

"Mystie, girl, where are you? Time to eat."

Even knowing that in my ghostly state, he probably wouldn't be able to see me—and I couldn't eat—I rushed to him out of habit and circled his ankles. He turned and his foot went right through me. It didn't hurt, the sensation equatable to fingers running through my fur, but it sent a shudder down my spine. I really was a ghost-cat, a dead-cat, a can't-eat-my-food-or-get-pets-from-Ryan-cat.

Ryan's eyes fell on my body. The food hit the floor, scattering everywhere. "Mystie?" He knelt beside me. I flitted to his side, wishing he could see me. Reaching out, he gave my tiny, still body a gentle shake. I didn't respond—well, my body didn't. The ghostly me rubbed against him, sinking into him ever so slightly.

"Oh, Myst." His voice cracked.

He sat there, staring at me, for a long while. Realizing my attempts to interact with him were getting no where, I waited in silent solidarity. Finally he picked himself up and fished his phone out of his pocket. He dialed and waited for an answer.

"Hey, Dad ... I can't come in today." He turned from my body. Ghost-me followed him as he left the kitchen and started digging through a closet. "No, I'm not sick. It's ... I'd rather not talk about it right now. Look, I know you can manage with just Carl today. When was the last time I took any sort of day off?... Uh-huh. Yeah. I'll be in tomorrow ... I'll tell you about it then. I've got to go, okay? ... Yeah, love ya, too. Bye." He slipped the phone into his pocket again, leaned against the closet door, and sighed.

When he returned to his searching a moment later, he produced a shoe box which he brought back to the kitchen. After wrapping my body in an old dish towel, he placed it in the box and took it out into the back yard. I didn't bother to follow at this point. No, I needed to think—to re-think. I didn't want to leave Ryan alone, but if he didn't even know I was there, how much good could I do him? None. No good at all. That stupid angel had tricked me.

I was sulking on the living room floor, staring at the TV, wishing my fish-program were on, when Ryan returned and slumped on the couch. Dirt streaked his coveralls, and his eyes looked a little red.

Half out of habit, I hopped up beside him and slipped onto his lap. His fingers absently tapped against the upholstery. I wanted to feel him run his fingers over my soft, gray fur, to have him scratch my chin, rub my ears, and bring me kitty treats. Instead, he sat. I sat. The morning ticked on.

This wasn't working—for either of us. What was I going to do?

After a bit, Ryan flipped on the TV. After a longer bit, he got up and made a sandwich but only ate a few bites. Mostly, he stared into space.

The light was fading outside when someone rapped on the door.

I followed Ryan to the entry. It was Carl and his wife, Jessie. Carl grinned and held up a foil-wrapped baking dish. "Hey, lil bro! My woman made lasagna! Want some?"

Ryan's eyebrows shot up. "What ...?" He let out a long breath and shrugged. "Sure. Come on in. I'll get some plates."

Jessie put her hand on his shoulder, stopping him from disappearing into the kitchen, though Carl brushed past, probably eager to get rid of the steaming baking dish. It *did* smell pretty good. Apparently I could still smell in ghost form. Did that mean I could taste?

Ryan shifted awkwardly under Jessie's stare.

"You okay?" Her eyes widened in motherly concern. She'd been pulling that face a lot. Carl and Jessie usually came over once a week to play that noisy game on the TV with all the running and screaming on the TV and eat pizza with Ryan. I liked Jessie but had noted that she had a lot less lap now than she had when I'd first met her—kittens, was my guess. I hope it wasn't a large litter. Human kittens are loud.

"I'm fine." It wasn't a convincing lie, even by human standards. Ryan's eyes dropped to his shoes as he said it.

"Why'd you call in to work today?" Carl called out from the kitchen. Ryan broke away from Jessie and hurried towards his brother. As he stepped onto the linoleum, cat food crunched under his feet.

"There's cat food all over the floor." Jessie stated the obvious. Humans like to do that. I don't know why.

Testing my theory, I pressed my tongue against the nearest piece of kibble. I could taste it, faintly, but couldn't get it off the floor and into my mouth. It might as well have been glued down. Frustrated I sat and licked my paws.

"Uh, yeah." Ryan darted to the broom closet then started to sweep up.

"Seriously, Ry, what's wrong?" Carl frowned at him.

Ryan paused, his fingers tightening around the broom handle. His cheeks reddened. "You'll think this is pathetic."

"Never," Jessie assured him. I noticed Carl didn't make any promises. Human big brothers are the worst.

Ryan cleared his throat. "It's just ... Mystie died this morning."

Jessie's jaw dropped. "Oh, Ryan, I'm so sorry!"

Carl arched an eyebrow. "Your cat?"

Jessie shot him a death glare.

Carl coughed. "Yeah, that's rough, man. Sorry."

"I get that she was just a cat, but she was my cat, you know? I've had her since before I moved into this place, nearly eleven years, and she's ...

she's part of my day-to-day. I'll be fine, really, but I didn't want to deal with work and people today."

"You take all the time you need." Jessie scurried across the room to hug him, stepping right on my tail. I flicked it out of the way, even though it didn't hurt.

"You know what you need? A good home cooked meal." Carl ripped the foil off the baking dish releasing a tantalizing scent of cheese and meat and tomato sauce. I hopped up onto the table and stuck my face into it. I couldn't get my mouth around it, of course, but the smell was heavenly, and for once no one tried to get me off the table. I guess that was one advantage of being a ghost cat.

The little family sat around the table, oblivious to me basking in the fragrance of the lasagna. It did feel rather awkward every time the spatula passed through my body to get another serving, but for the joy of resting on a bed of succulent pasta and meat sauce, I'd accept that.

After dinner, however, Jessie replaced the foil and stuck the dish in the fridge. I thought about testing my ability to walk through doors, but as I could still sense temperature, just as I could still smell and taste, I didn't savor the idea of getting into the cold fridge, even if it meant staying near my beloved lasagna. Instead, I followed the humans into the living room.

"Want to play a game?" Carl motioned towards the TV and attached console. He sat on the floor and reached for a controller, obviously expecting a yes.

"You and Jess can if you want, but I'm not in the mood." Ryan settled onto the couch.

Jessie sat on the floor next to her husband and leaned back into him. Carl grimaced and put the controller back before wrapping his arms around her. "Still the cat, huh? I mean, I get it. I love animals, but you had to know she was getting old, and she was just an animal—"

Jessie playfully slapped Carl's arm. "Says the man who cries at the end of any movie where the dog dies."

He chuckled. "Got me there, I guess."

Ryan rubbed his legs. I hopped onto the couch beside him and butted my head against his shoulder.

I'd been right. He wasn't handling my absence well. He needed me. That stupid angel was wrong—but she'd also left me in a position where I couldn't do anything to fix the problem. Come to think of it, was I really sure she was an angel? This trick seemed more fitting for someone of a less heavenly origin.

"Is there anything we can do?" Jessie asked.

Ryan sighed. "No, not really. It means a lot that you're here right now, but I know I can't monopolize all your evenings. I suppose I'll eventually head down to the shelter. I mean, I have a half a bag of cat food and two months' supply of kitty litter, not to mention that I just like cats."

I shuddered, my stomach flipflopping. Was he going to replace me so easily?

"It feels disloyal, though, thinking of that so soon, after she gave me so many years." He tapped his fingers on the arm of the couch. My innards settled. That was my Ryan, a respectful young man if ever there was one. Still, maybe I shouldn't have been rooting against him getting another cat. Another cat might help him not be so alone, and there didn't seem to be a way for me to get back to him.

"If you don't mind me saying so, Ry, I don't think you need a cat." Carl smirked and gave Jessie a squeeze. "You haven't dated in years. Not seriously, anyway."

Ryan dropped his eyes. "I'm just not into online dating or app dating, and when you work as much as I do—"

"Oh, bull." Carl snorted. "Considering the fact that you named your cat after your highschool sweetheart, I think you've got a deeper hangup than 'too busy to bother with the dating thing.'"

My ears twitched. I was named after a girlfriend?

"Mystie was named after your high school sweetheart?" Jessie leaned forward.

"They dated from freshman year on, only for her to dump him at graduation because she didn't want to be seen with a guy who wasn't going to college."

"It wasn't like that!" Ryan jumped up. "I mean ... it was because of college, but because she was going, not because I wasn't. I mean ... long distance would've been hard." He rubbed the back of his neck. "And I didn't name Mystie after Misty. She had that name at the shelter and I... I don't know. I thought it was a sign."

"Okay, sure." Carl softened his tone. "Look, all I'm saying, bro, is that if you're looking at the shelter, you're chasing after the wrong sort of—Ouch!" He recoiled as Jessie elbowed him—hard. "Wrong sort of female companionship!" He held up his hands. A mischievous glint crept into his eyes. "What did you think I was going to say?"

"Men." She sniffed.

I curled into a tight ball. Come to think of it, I'd never seen Ryan with a human female outside of his family. Carl had brought a few women to family dinners over the years before eventually settling on Jessie, but Ryan—no. It had always been me and him. Did he need a mate too? Did he want to start having litters of human-kittens?

Ryan slumped onto the couch again. "Maybe you're right. It's not that I'm against the idea, but it's also not like I can order myself a girlfriend with two day shipping."

"Maybe from Russia." Carl scoffed.

"Must you make everything into a bad joke." Jessie clicked her tongue before focusing on Ryan. "We can introduce you to someone. I have friends—"

"I appreciate the offer, but I don't need you guys to set me up." Ryan bit his bottom lip. "I know women ... I think." His brow furrowed. Based on what I knew about his life, I wasn't so sure, but if there's one thing I've learned about humans, they can convince themselves of pretty much anything.

"What about that cute girl you said moved in next door a few months ago?" Carl leaned back comfortably. "Did you ever get the courage up to introduce yourself?"

Jessie sat a little straighter, her eyes widening. "You have a cute neighbor?"

Ryan's ears glowed crimson. "Why do I tell you anything, Carl? We met once when we had some mail mix up. Yeah, she was cute, but I don't really know her, and it's not like I can just go knock on her door."

"Why can't you?"

"She'll think I'm a creeper!"

"Yeah, talking to her twice in three months. That's obviously stalker material." Carl rolled his eyes.

I swished my tail back and forth, trying to remember the neighbor in question. It had to be the woman in the house on the right. From window watching—mostly for birds, but if people wandered into my field of vision, I'd observe them too—I knew the majority of neighbors by sight. The house to our left was an elderly couple with a small dog who barked a lot. The house across the street was a family with a mini-van full of noisy human-kittens. The house to our right had a youngish woman who I had only ever seen leave or enter the house alone. Yes, that was what I'd do. I'd have to get my human and that human together.

Something tickled at the back of my neck, and I spun around to stare out the window.

There stood the angel. How dare she watch my private time with my human and his family?

Rage rose within me. Baring my teeth, I rushed at her, hit the wall, and slipped right through it as if it had been a soap bubble. Skidding to a halt on the other side, I shook myself off. I guess I could go through walls, though I probably should've tried at a slower speed for the first time. Oh well. I'd act as if I'd done that on purpose.

She crossed her arms. "You ready to go yet?"

"You said you'd give me a month! It hasn't even been a day!" I snarled.

"I'm not making you go. Just checking in on you. After a few months on this job, you learn how indecisive cats can be. First they don't want to go, then they do want to go, then they change their minds, and you're standing there with the pearly gates open, tapping your toes as they sit and flick their tail." She sighed. "So, you're not ready to go?"

"I told you, he *needs* me." I stuck my chest out. Settling into the yard, I could vaguely feel the cold of the evening air and the dampness of the grass beneath me, but it didn't bother me as much as it had in life.

"Well, you aren't doing him much good now, are you?" The angel arched a snow-white eyebrow.

"Only because you tricked me. You didn't say I'd have no way to interact with him. Can't ghosts move things? Make noises? They can in all the stories, anyway."

She winced. "So you're officially requesting to be upgraded to a level two haunting?"

"Yes!" I said quickly, though I had no idea what that was.

She got down on her hands and knees to look me in the eye. "I'll level with you, cat, I do have the authority to give you that upgrade, but it's not something I offer lightly. Usually only when there's life and limb on the line for the kitty cat's unfinished business."

"What is life and limb compared to the heart?" I allowed my whiskers to tremble ever so sincerely.

The angel groaned. "There are rules to a level two haunting. A spirit allowed to linger for a level one is given the power to observe and can leave the haunt at any time. A level two, you get interaction upgrades.

You can move objects with some effort, make noises the living can hear—again with some effort—but there's a catch, a cost. You will *not* be able to return home until the sworn purpose of your haunting—the unfinished business, if you will—is completely finished."

I hesitated. "What happens if I *don't* finish the unfinished business?"

"Then you stay. You stay as long as it takes, even if that's until the end of the world. I won't tell you how many pets have gotten stuck moving curtains and squeaking floorboards for the rest of eternity because they signed onto a level two haunt but weren't able to close the deal on whatever it was they wanted to do." She narrowed her gaze. "So, cat, how sure are you that you can do whatever it is you want to do? And is the risk of not doing it worth potentially centuries of flitting about between lives?"

A cold shiver ran down my spine. This was all getting super serious, super fast, and I wasn't super ready.

"Give me a second." I slipped through the wall as if pushing aside a curtain. On the other side, Ryan sat on the couch, a dark shadow in the otherwise cheery living room, his eyes distant. He deserved companionship. He didn't deserve to be alone. Steeling myself, I walked through the sheetrock and aluminum siding again, stuck my nose as high in the air as I could manage, and stared down the angel. "I'll do it. Upgrade me to a level two haunt."

The angel reached out and released a shower of a flaky substance that had a faint scent of catnip. My eyes might've crossed just a little bit. The world went hazy, and when I came to, the angel was gone and the living room behind me was dark and empty.

Sneaking back inside, I decided to see if this "level two" haunt thing actually worked or was just another trick. I sighted one of my toys, a purple plastic ball with a bell inside, wedged beneath the couch. Crouching down, I batted at it. My paw sank right through. Disappointment gripped me. Then I remembered. The angel had said

I could move things *with effort*. In all fairness, I had put absolutely no effort into batting at that ball. Focusing on my limbs, I imagined them being solid. I imagined my paw making contact with the toy and sending it flying across the room. My muscles ached in response. I clenched my jaw and swung.

The ball rolled out from under the couch and about a foot across the carpet. I flattened myself into the floor and took a deep breath. That had taken more out of me than expected, but maybe I needed to build up my stamina. If anything, it was a start.

Not wanting to stress myself any more that night, I wandered into the bedroom. Ryan lay in bed, eyes closed. As I watched he fitfully rolled from his back to his side, then back again. I hopped up onto the bed and settled against his side. I put all my strength and will into simply purring. The noise reverberated through the room, and Ryan lay still.

The next morning Ryan left for work as normal, though anyone who knew him could've seen he wasn't his usual, good-natured self. Slower in his movements, kept glancing at my abandoned food bowl as he sipped his coffee, sighed often. The poor guy didn't like being alone, and it was up to me to fix that.

Remembering what he'd said about meeting the neighbor previously due to a mail mix-up, I had an immediate plan for how to bring them together, but first, I thought I'd check her out, see if she was good enough for my human in the first place. As soon as Ryan's car pulled away from the curb, I bounced through the front door and across the porch.

The neighbor's car still sat in front of her place. She definitely worked away from home—I'd seen her go back and forth in those pajama-looking clothes people wore at my vet's office sometimes—but it looked like she hadn't left yet. I zipped through the fence. Running at solid barriers at full speed was almost second nature now. I rather liked the gentle "popping" sensation that happened when I burst through a wall or a door or a human being's legs. With a leap to clear the foundation, I broke through the exterior wall of the neighbor's house and skidded to a halt inside a warm, cheery living room.

The neighbor apparently had a thing for color. The couch was lime-green. The curtains were blue with a pineapple pattern on them. I strolled over to the TV. She owned a gaming console similar to Ryan's and it looked like the pictures on some of the game boxes were the same too. He'd like that. It seemed to be his primary way of engaging with other humans, sitting in front of TVs pushing buttons. She also had a shelf of movies and four times that many of books. Homebody, then? Again, like my Ryan.

"What are you doing in here?"

My tail nearly hit the ceiling. Landing on all fours, I spun around to face a bulky, brown tabby with accusing amber eyes.

My jaw dropped. "You can see me?"

"Well, duh." He sat down and licked his front paw.

I glanced around. Had upgrading to a level two haunting made me visible? No, Ryan hadn't seen me at all that morning.

"But ... but I'm dead."

"Yeah, I noticed that. Bummer, isn't it?" The tabby stretched two lanky fore-legs forward and leaned into a massive yawn.

"But you can see me?" I tilted my head.

The strange cat winked. "I'm psychic."

My eyes widened. "Really?"

He snorted. "No. Geez, you must not have got out much when you were alive. All cats can see ghosts. You've never noticed something and stared at it only to have your human freak out because they thought nothing was there?"

My ears twitched as I considered this. "Sometimes, but it was always with bugs or birds, and I just assumed humans weren't that observant."

"Bugs and birds can be ghosts too ... in fact, considering how often bugs drop dead, the majority of bugs I've seen are ghosts, I think."

I guess that made sense ... and explained that time a house wren sat on top of our fridge scolding me for a week and Ryan did absolutely nothing about it. Come to think of it, that wren had been slightly transparent.

"What are you doing in here?" the cat asked.

I curled my tail around my paws, considering him. Strange cats, like strange humans, couldn't always be trusted, but if he lived in this house, then neighbor-woman was most likely his human. If I needed to find out about a human, I wouldn't find a better source than her cat.

"My name's Mystie, and I'm on a bit of a mission."

"Do tell?" The cat's ears swiveled in my direction.

Pushing aside the last of my hesitancy, I told him about Ryan. About how he needed me, but how the stupid angel had ruined that. How I'd bargained with the angel to bring Ryan a new companion before I moved on.

"Well don't look at me." The tabby yawned again. "I have a human, and I'm not leaving her for your Ryan."

I rolled my eyes. "I'm not here after you, tuna-breath. I'm investigating your human."

"Oh." He froze mid-stretch. "*That* sort of companion. Why didn't you say so? Come on. I have something to show you." He waltzed over to the book shelf. "My name's Shawn, by the way." The bottom shelf was full of DVDs instead of books. He put his paw on the first and pulled it off. "*While You Were Sleeping.*" The second DVD case hit the carpet. "*The Wedding Planner.*" Another one toppled at his nudging. "*You've Got Mail, Hitch, No Reservations...*"

I eyed the glossy covers and the unnaturally attractive humans staring back at me from them. "What are these?"

"Yeah, your human is definitely a single guy." He sniffed. "These, my ghostly friend, are rom coms. Romantic comedies. Chick flicks.

They're what she binges every Valentine's Day while hugging me way too tight and getting chocolate in my fur." He kicked at the boxes with his hind legs as if he were tossing litter over them. "What I'm trying to say is, my human might need yours just as much as yours needs mine, and I'll be happy to help your Ryan meet my Violet if that's what it takes to get her someone else to watch these ridiculous things with."

"I think Ryan prefers movies with lasers." I wasn't quite sure what such movies were called, but I knew lasers, and most of the movies he liked had lasers.

"Oh, she likes those too." He motioned towards a section on the end of the shelf that had some more familiar looking covers. "Though not on Valentine's Day or after two glasses of that smelly red stuff she drinks on weekends. Then it's all rom coms and sniffling into my fur about how she's lucky to have at least one man in her life, even if he's four-legged."

Footsteps tromped towards us, and while my brain knew I was invisible, some instinct sent me skittering behind the nearest side table.

Violet—which was apparently 'cute neighbor's' name—bent down and rubbed Shawn's ears.

"I've got to go to work now, boy. I'll see you this evening. It's pizza night, and you know what that means?"

"Tuna." The word rumbled as a purr through Shawn.

"Tuna!" Violet grinned. "Yeah, you know tuna, doncha, boy? You know so many words. You're such a smart boy."

"Gag me with a litter shovel," I mumbled.

Shawn flicked his tail in my general direction but kept his eyes on Violet until she left the room. He then spun to face me. "So, what's your plan?"

I explained about the mail mix up that had previously brought them together and how I hoped it could happen again.

"Huh." He scratched behind his ears. Shawn was kind of fidgety for a full-grown feline. "It will work to get them face-to-face, but that happened before and they didn't follow through, you know? It doesn't do much good to pounce on a mouse if you aren't ready to sink your teeth into it."

"Well, before Ryan had *me*," I pointed out. "So he didn't need Violet. Now he does. I'm sure he'll do whatever it is humans do when they want to mate."

"According to those dumb movies, it involves a lot of tripping and falling, sometimes wardrobe malfunctions."

I had no idea what a wardrobe malfunction was. Sometimes it didn't seem like Shawn was speaking cat.

"Well, whatever it is. I'm sure he'll do it." I hesitated. It seemed like Violet was a good human. She took the time to say good-bye to Shawn before she left the house, after all. That meant, like Ryan, she valued her feline companion. Not the type to insist on abandoning a cat due to babies and moving.

A deep sadness crept through me. I liked to say I didn't care about that. About those humans who left me. After all, I found Ryan. I had a happy life. Still, there's a part of a cat's soul that never gets over being left behind. A human who wouldn't do that, a human who stuck with you, no matter what life threw at them, that was a good human, and good humans deserved happiness.

What could help Ryan and Violet find each other and stick, though? How could Ryan know Violet was a good human? Obviously, by seeing that she had an undeniably good-human trait: the love of cats.

"If Ryan knows she has a cat, it'd probably help."

He cocked his head to one side. "Oh, yeah, I bet it would. I can't imagine how hard it must be for humans, meeting other humans but not knowing for sure if they have cats." He gave a slow nod. "If you can get the mail switched up, I can see to the cat thing, all right?"

"Deal."

I endured the next several hours staring out the window, waiting for the mail truck. Shawn spent that time blabbing on and on and on about his many exploits and the other ghosts he'd met—mostly birds, but there'd been an old stray who died in the alley behind his house and had chosen to linger for a week to see what it was like inside a home.

"Nice old guy. A little skittish, but understandably considering his life. Felt sorry that he'd never had a person, but glad to keep him company before he passed over."

It bugged me a little, hearing about other cats choosing to stay. The angel's rant had given me some idea that I wasn't unique in my stubbornness, but I didn't like to think I was a cliché either. At least the street stray hadn't insisted on a level two haunt. I was still unusual for that.

Finally the little white truck rattled up to the mailbox. I stiffened. What if the mail carrier didn't have any mail for either Violet or Ryan today? Thankfully, the postal worker opened Violet's box and slipped in a small stack of white envelopes and one pink one. I relaxed. Now to wait until no one was watching and make the switch.

The mission proved harder than anticipated. While I could slip through walls easily enough, and even hop up and into the mailbox, when I tried to drag the mail out with me, it stuck against the door. Apparently while I could move objects, I couldn't pull them through solid barriers. It took some finagling, but I finally got open the mailbox, pushed out the pink envelope, then jumped out after it. I couldn't figure out a way to close the box after me, so I left it hanging open.

Thankfully, Ryan didn't have a mailbox. His house had one of those old fashioned mail slots in the door. I dragged Violet's envelope down the street, pausing anytime a car passed in case it saw the envelope moving against the wind and stopped to investigate. It took a lot more effort to move things as a ghost—level two haunting or not. By the time I reached Ryan's porch, every tuft of fur ached. Somehow, I managed to grab the paper in my teeth, lift it up, and shove it through the mail slot. I then melted through the door and collapsed next to it to await Ryan's return.

I drifted into what, if I'd still been alive, I would've called a nap, though as a spirit it was more a hazy sensation that distracted me from the passage of time. The sound of a car pulling up roused me from my stupor. From the shadows reaching across the entryway, it was early evening. Also, shadows aside, that was when Ryan usually got home, and I recognized the sound of his car. The car door slammed shut. The footsteps clomped up the porch steps. I stood on top of the small stack of mail—Violet's stolen letter as well as a few items the mail carrier had left for Ryan—and waited.

Ryan opened the door and paused. Normally this would've been when I'd rushed to him, eager for my nightly pets plus my evening meal. I meowed and rubbed up against his ankles, but not wanting to spook him, I didn't put enough effort into it to manifest into the physical realm.

With a sigh, Ryan bent down and picked up the letters before shuffling into the kitchen.

Ears perked, I followed him, waiting to see what would happen when he noticed that the top envelope wasn't addressed to him. Annoyingly, he set all the mail down on the kitchen table before opening the fridge and staring into it for several minutes.

After a bit, he pulled out the leftover lasagna, slapped a spatula full of it onto a paper plate, and sat at the table while it spun around in the microwave, sporadically spattering bursts of tomato sauce onto the window. He aimlessly flipped through his phone, not even glancing at the envelopes. Every inch of my—not body? Incorporeal being? Well, whatever I was made up of in that moment, it itched.

Still a little tired from straining myself to get the envelope in the house, I hopped next to the stack and batted at it with my paw. Not enough to move it, but so that the paper "crinkled" under my touch. Ryan jolted in his chair.

At that moment, the microwave beeped. He got up and retrieved the steaming lasagna, which he poked at with a fork before setting it to the side to cool. My tail twitched as he reached for the mail.

He separated the first two envelopes with barely a glance, mumbling something about only ever getting junk. The third, however, was the envelope from Violet's box. I'd picked it because, as well as being conspicuously pink, it was more "square" and "stiff" than the other ones, which I thought might mean it was important.

"A card?" He frowned. "Who would send me a card." Not even flipping it to the side with the address, he slid his finger under the flap and popped it open. He pulled out a flowery picture and opened it. Another slip of paper fell to the tabletop as he read, "Happy birthday ... Granddaughter?" His eyes widened, and he snatched up the envelope. With one glance at the address, he flushed and stuck the card back in the envelope. "Stupid, stupid ... why the heck ... and a check too! Dang it, she'll think I'm a thief." Gathering it all together he bolted for the door, then froze with his hand on the knob. The corners of his mouth twitched, and he gazed down at the envelope.

I could see his brain thinking. I knew my human. How shy he was. How afraid someone would misinterpret what he was doing as a "bad thing." How he'd do anything to avoid an awkward confrontation. What if she thought he'd stolen the card? Should he put it back in the mailbox so he wouldn't have to talk to her? Pretend the whole thing had never happened?

Come on, Ryan. You can do this. You can talk to the girl.

Letting out a whistling breath, Ryan opened the door. The sun hovered over the houses across the street, the sky scraped with tones of orange and pink, as he reached her front door and lightly knocked. He didn't notice me tagging at his heels.

The door opened. Violet was a petite human with olive skin and boisterous dark curls. If she'd been a cat, she would've been a Persian, dainty with a round face and tiny nose. She'd changed out of her work-pajamas into what I assumed were real pajamas and a pair of fuzzy slippers with kitty ears and googly eyes. Ignoring the lifeless gaze of her slippers, I peered around her, hoping that Shawn remembered his part of the plan.

Ryan shifted from foot to foot. "Uh, hi, I'm your neighbor."

"Yeah, Ryan, right?" She smiled. "We met that time I got your electric bill by mistake."

"Yeah, that's me, and it happened again, well, not a bill." He held up the card. "Sorry, I opened it before I saw it was for you. Uh … happy birthday?"

"Oh, it's early!" She snatched it like an eager child after a lollipop, then flushed, seeming to realize her lack of decorum. "Sorry. She always sends me a check for my birthday, and I know what I'm going to do with it for months before it gets here. There's a game I've been waiting to order until this is in my account." She dropped her gaze. "I guess that's pretty pathetic, a grown woman waiting for her grandma to send her money to buy a video game, but nursing school put me in a debt hole I'm only just starting to work my way out of."

"I actually think it's awesome your priorities are a new game. I can understand that. When I first moved out of my parents' and money was still tight, I'd squirrel away a bit of each paycheck for the same reason."

I gave an impatient meow. Where was that slacker Shawn?

"Yes, well, thank you for bringing my card back." She fiddled with the envelope. "I've had mail stolen out of my mailbox and packages off my porch multiple times since I moved in here."

"Yeah, that happens." He glanced down the street. "I'd like to say it's a great neighborhood, and don't get me wrong, there are some good people here, but I installed a security camera on my porch for a reason. Too many boxes going missing. I don't even think it's neighbors, just people driving by and seeing an opportunity."

"Well, it doesn't make a woman living alone feel very safe." She frowned, rubbing her arms as if she were cold. I slipped through her legs.

"Shawn!" I hissed. "Why aren't you here?"

The stupid tabby stuck his head around a corner down the hall. "Chill out, will you. They're doing good. Let them build a little chemistry. Geez, you really haven't watched a single rom com, have you?"

"I mean, if someone were to break in here, I have a baseball bat, but I think most home invaders would laugh, and do you know how long it takes 9-1-1 to get the cops to this part of town?" Violet continued.

"Yeah, that would make me nervous too. You know, if you want my number, I'm right next door. I'm not as useful as the police, but my response time would be way faster."

She hesitated. "I mean, it might be good to have, in case I have to go out of town and need someone who can collect my mail ... or the other way around. I'd be happy to collect your mail if you went on vacation."

They both pulled out phones and fiddled with them, talking numbers and stuff.

"Shawn, they're running out of small talk!" I snarled. "Get your tail down here!"

"Bossy." He slunk down the hall in no particular hurry, bumped up against Violet's legs, and gave a deep, throaty "Meerrrowww."

Ryan jerked and braced himself against the doorway. "Oh ... you have a cat?"

"Yep." She grinned and stooped down to scoop Shawn up. "This is my Shawnie-boy. He's kind of my baby." She pressed him into her cheek.

Ryan's jaw worked for a little bit as if he'd bitten into a tough piece of steak and couldn't decide whether to spit it out or swallow. Finally he rasped out, "He's ... great."

Her brow furrowed. "Yeah, he is. You want to pet him?" She held him out.

Shawn glanced down at me. "You better be grateful."

"Shut up and accept your pets," I sniffed.

Ryan ran his hand over Shawn's forehead and down his neck. "He's nice. I ... I better get home."

I deflated. My plan to introduce him to a fellow cat lover had somehow backfired.

"Oh, yeah." Violet's shoulders slumped. I don't think she wanted Ryan to go either. "Well, now that we know each other, we should try not to be strangers. I'll definitely feel safer having your number tonight, especially with the date."

"The date?" He frowned.

"Oh, not this again," Shawn groaned.

"What?" I whispered.

"It's Friday ... the thirteenth." She shivered. "I always get a little spooked about that."

"Last time she watched a scary movie and then insisted our refrigerator was possessed for a week." Shawn flicked his ears in disgust. "It's not—The printer in the office is, but the fridge is fine."

I wasn't sure if he was serious, so I ignored him.

Ryan laughed. "Huh. Well, if you see any ghoulies lurking, don't hesitate to call me."

With that he left, and Violet shut the door behind him. She released Shawn.

"He seems nice," she said. "You want some tuna, boy?"

Shawn's ears perked up, and he meowed.

I sulked after them to the kitchen. Normally the sound of a can opener was music to my ears, but now, it might as well have been the barking of dogs for how little joy it brought me. I glared at Shawn as he ate.

"What are you so grumpy about?" he asked between massive gulps of tuna. "They hit it off, didn't they?"

"Until Ryan limped away." I settled into cat-loaf formation, paws tucked beneath my body, tail wrapped tightly around the whole of me.

"You can't expect it to happen over night ... though if a 'ghoulie' shows up, maybe she'll give him a call." He laughed and nearly choked on his dinner.

I bared my teeth at him then it struck me. A purr rumbled through me, and I settled back into my loaf, smirking at Shawn.

He paused, mouth half-opened, tuna juices dribbling down his chin. "I don't like that look."

"A ghoulie *will* show up tonight. That ghoulie is me."

Shawn swallowed his tuna, his tail swaying like a serpent. "You're evil. I like it."

It turned out Shawn's human wanted to watch a rom com that night. I don't know if this was a good or bad sign, but she poured herself a glass of something red, made a comment about tomorrow being her day off, and settled under a fleece blanket to sip and watch. I tried to watch too—Shawn thought it might be educational—but found myself dozing off while the couple was still in what Shawn called the 'cute bickering' stage. When I woke up two attractive humans were hugging on a city street in spite of various people wandering by them. Maybe this is normal for humans?

Violet set her now empty glass on the side table and collected Shawn off the couch beside her. "Someday, maybe that'll be me," she whispered before turning towards the bedroom.

Apparently Shawn slept in Violet's room. She shut the door with him inside, leaving the rest of the house to me.

Now was the time to act.

While I didn't have any personal experience with hauntings, some of Ryan's game involved ghosts and zombies that jumped out at him, so I had a general idea of what scared humans. While I couldn't make myself look big and scary, I definitely could make things go bump in the night. I hopped onto the bookshelf, selected a particularly good sized hard back, and nudged it. It wibbled, wobbled, and fell to the floor below with a clunk.

No response from the bedroom.

Sniffing, I moseyed into the kitchen. A water glass sat next to the sink. Ah, that would make a decent crash. Alighting next to it, I butted it with my head. It shattered on the floor with a satisfying crunch and clink.

Silence. Then a door creaked open. After a dramatic pause, I sent a plate after the glass.

"Eeep!" a muffled voice echoed down the hall. Lights flipped on, casting long shadows into the kitchen. Footsteps squeaked towards me. Then, baseball bat in hand, a shivering Violet peered into the kitchen. She gaped at the broken dishes, glanced around the room, then ran to the front door. I heard her jiggle the handle. Still locked, she was sure to discover. She then hurried in the opposite direction, probably to a back door.

Shawn wandered into the kitchen. "Nice start. She's pretty spooked."

"I haven't even started yet." I winked.

We followed Violet around the house for several minutes as she checked windows and looked in closets. Finally she settled on the couch, one hand clutching her phone, her baseball bat across her lap. She shuddered.

"Hold up. Got some comforting to do." Shawn bolted from my side and rubbed against hers. She absently ran her fingers down his spine.

"Condensation. Condensation builds up under the dishes and they slide across the counter tops, like those rocks in the desert, you know?" she whispered. "Yeah, that's it."

"She's talking herself out of it," Shawn said.

"On it." I rushed across the room, tangled myself in the curtains and started to rock from side to side.

Violet gasped.

"Ooh, very dramatic. I like it," Shawn said. "Try the TV next. The red button on the remote."

Violet ran over and gave the curtains a tug, sending me rolling onto the carpet, but of course she couldn't see me.

Shawn nudged the remote, which sat on the arm of the couch, with his nose. "If I do it she'll catch on." He scampered to sit on the opposite side of the couch as I settled next to the remote. I pressed the "on" button.

The TV crackled to life with an all too perky voice attempting to sell some gold coins. Violet spun about, hands in front of her face. "What the heck!"

I tapped another button, changing the channel to an obnoxious cartoon dog making implausible faces, then again to a woman in a dark house screaming. Violet screamed too. She dashed to the TV and pressed the power button. I hopped down.

"You think she'll call him yet?" I asked.

As if in answer, Violet snatched her phone off the couch cushion only to freeze. She glanced at Shawn. "He'll think I'm crazy. Am I crazy? Did you see that too?"

Shawn gave a sympathetic meow then glanced at me. "Let me stare at you. That always freaks humans out." He fixed me with a steady gaze.

Violet's mouth dropped open as she watched him watching me.

"Shawn?" she whispered. "What are you looking at?"

"Yep, works every time." Shawn chuckled.

"She's not dialing," I observed.

"Yeah, the 'don't want to seem nuts' instinct is strong with the humans." He rolled his eyes, not a visible movement to humans. Cats seem expressionless to most of them, I've noticed, but as a cat I know when a cat is rolling his eyes.

"She needs to get over it and dial that dang phone."

Violet continued to gape at Shawn who kept his eyes glued on me, occasionally letting out a nervous, "Chirp."

Well, time to escalate. Throwing back my head and summoning all my energy, I gave forth a blood-curdling, whisker-curling, fur-ruffling yowl.

Violet tripped over her own two feet trying to scurry away and landed hard on her rump.

"Vi!" Shawn leaped from the couch onto her lap.

"What was that?" she wailed.

My whole being felt thin and weak, like watered-down milk, but I managed to give out a rasping meow ending with a hiss strong enough for Violet to hear. She shuddered and snatched up her phone, dialing faster than I would've thought humanly possible—humans being rather on the clumsy side.

"Hello?" Ryan's voice echoed through the phone.

"Something's in my house!" she all but wept.

"What's in your house?"

"Something! I ... I ... I don't know. It's awful. Please help!"

A little lightheaded from all the paranormal effort, I angled my body towards her living room window, which faced Ryan's house. The porch light flipped on, and I saw Ryan booking it out the door in our general direction. I let myself slump onto the couch cushions in a weary heap.

Violet hurried to the door and let him in. Between sobs, she frantically tried to explain what had happened, even showing him the broken dishes.

"It sounds like some sort of animal must have got inside."

"An invisible animal that screams like a banshee?" she snapped. "It was making the most awful noises, and I couldn't see anything."

He got down on his hands and knees. "Maybe it's under the couch?"

"Careful!" she gasped. "What if it's some sort of rabid possum?"

Ryan just chuckled.

It was then that I realized my mistake. I'd spent so much effort convincing Violet without even thinking that I might need to convince Ryan. My legs wobbled beneath me, but I somehow managed to get back on my paws.

"Nothing under here." He stood and rubbed the back of his neck. "Do you mind if I check the rest of the house? I won't feel great about leaving you alone until I'm sure it's safe."

Violet went pale at the words "leaving you alone," but she nodded. "I hate to inconvenience you ... but I'm terrified." Picking up the baseball bat, she followed him down the hall. I heard the creak of door hinges as they inspected the hall closet.

"You all right?" Shawn tilted his head.

"Just tired. I need to make some sort of show."

Shawn nudged the remote control towards me. "Here you go. Wait until I'm out of the room. He might think I did it if I'm in here when it happens." With that Shawn darted off.

I counted to five to give Shawn plenty of time to get away then pressed down on the power button.

The TV flickered on. The black and white woman on the screen screamed bloody murder. Something crashed down the hall, and Ryan rushed into the living room, Violet close behind him. He stared at the TV.

"It did it again!" Tears brimmed from Violet's eyes, and I almost regretted how much I'd put her through tonight—almost. I mean, it was all for a good cause. If she knew what I was doing, and why, she'd probably thank me ... probably.

"That's weird." Ryan gave a low whistle and switched off the late night movie.

A large thump echoed down the hall. Both humans jumped—towards each other. Violet collided against Ryan's chest as he grabbed her about the waist. Immediately, she flushed and he jerked away, stammering. Consumed in their awkwardness, they didn't notice Shawn slipping into the room.

"That was you?" I asked.

He nodded. "Potted plant in the office. I've been itching for an excuse to knock it off the shelf. Thanks for that." He licked his paws, dislodging a bit of stray potting soil.

"I can't stay here!" Violet stammered. "There's something going on. Something's trying to get me!" She took her phone out of her pocket and touched the virtual assistant button. "Hotels under a hundred dollars, please."

"You don't need to do that." Ryan exhaled. "Look, I have a spare room. It's all furnished because I have out of town cousins who stay with me sometimes. There's even a lock on the inside, if that makes you more comfortable."

She stiffened. "I couldn't impose like that."

"It's not a big deal. Honestly, I don't think I'll be able to sleep after ... after all this." He let out a long breath. "My brother used to spook the heck out of me with ghost stories, and this is hitting all the tropes."

Shawn settled next to me. While I couldn't quite touch him, I could vaguely feel his weight and warmth, and it comforted me in my weakened state. I needed it. Too wiped out to do any more "haunting," the rest of the evening was up to the humans.

"They better not screw this up," I mumbled.

"I ... I can't leave Shawn," Violet gave a weak protest.

"That's fine. I even have a litter box."

Her eyes widened. "You have a cat!" Violet's expression brightened, and she bounced on her toes.

"Yes ... No ... I mean ..." He cleared his throat. "I did until yesterday morning. She passed away. I haven't done anything with her stuff yet. It's all just sort of there."

"Oh." Violet touched his arm. "You poor thing. What happened?"

"Old, I guess. I'd had her since I was eighteen ... almost eleven years, and I think she was three or four when I adopted her." His voice came out husky. "I knew she was slowing down for a while, but somehow it still blindsided me."

"That's a long time. I bet you gave her a good life."

"I did my best." He smiled weakly.

My ears flattened against my head. I wished I could tell him I was there, looking out for him, trying to get him to do something good for himself for a change, but I couldn't, so instead I reached over and tapped the remote again.

A blaring infomercial jolted the humans together again, Ryan grabbing Violet's shoulder, her cringing against him.

"Grab your stuff. I'll get your cat," he hissed.

"I should play hard to get, but I won't for your sake, Mystie." Shawn sniffed as Ryan scooped him up.

"He's good with cats. Give him a break." I flicked my tail at Shawn. Such a diva. Were all males like that? I was glad Ryan had kept me an only cat. I wouldn't have been able to stand living with a ham like Shawn.

A minute later, Violet hurried out of the back room with a dufflebag. "Got enough for the night. I feel awful making you go through all this."

"No worries." Ryan traded Shawn for the bag.

"You coming with us?" Shawn called out as Violet switched off the living room lights and the still blaring TV.

I tried to stand, but my legs buckled. "I'll be around in a bit. Keep an eye on those two for me, all right?"

"I'm on the case." Shawn winked as the humans whisked out of the room, cat in tow. The front door slammed shut, and Violet's house fell silent.

I saw the lights come on in Ryan's kitchen. Shadows moved against the walls. They were probably too wound up to settle in for the night.

Good. That meant they'd keep talking. In a few minutes, hopefully, my strength would return, and I'd get a chance to supervise their unofficial first date.

"Well, you did it."

My fur puffed up, and my ears flattened against my head as the angel materialized before me.

"I should know better than to be surprised by now." She clicked her tongue. "You cats tend to get your way, no matter how ridiculous it is."

"They just met, though," I pointed out. "What if it doesn't work out?"

"Oh, I got some insight from the Big Man." She pointed towards the ceiling. "This ends well, apparently with four kids, twelve grandkids, and a series of spoiled cats." She eased herself onto the couch beside me and ran her hand down my spine. "You've set up a legacy with your unselfish devotion to your human, Mystie. Now, please. Let me take you to some well-deserved rest."

I shrank away. "No! I'm not ready to go! Ryan still ... he needs ... I mean ... I need him." My throat tightened, and I found I couldn't look at her any more.

Unselfish? I wasn't unselfish. Yes, I wanted Ryan to be happy, but more than that, I didn't want to leave Ryan. I didn't want to say good-bye to the one person who had thought I was something special, who had given me a home, and who had always been there for me. Whatever this "well-deserved rest" involved, it couldn't be as good as Ryan.

"It's only for a while, my sweet girl," the angel soothed. "Humans take longer to reach the finish line, but the destination is the same. It's not forever. In the meantime, there are new friends to make, sunbeams to sleep in. It'll be all right. I promise."

My tail drooped. "Can I say good-bye?"

Her face softened. "That sounds like a fine idea." She blinked out of view.

Almost immediately, my strength returned. I suspected she'd done something to replenish it, but I didn't want to hurry even if I now could. After a quick circuit around Violet's house, admiring Shawn's work with the toppled houseplant in the office, I stepped onto the porch and stared up at the night sky. A pale full moon gazed down at me. The beams from it shimmered through my being, filling me with light and sparkle until I felt lovely enough to dance among the stars. I darted down the sidewalk and rushed through the front door into the house where I'd spent so many happy years.

A faint scent of popcorn drifted from the kitchen, and the soundtrack of a movie echoed from the living room. I peeked my head into the kitchen first. Shawn was there, shamelessly snacking from *my* food bowl.

I glared at him. "Enjoying yourself?"

He stopped mid-chew. "Oh, hi." He swallowed. "Wondered when you'd show up. They seem to be hitting it off. Decided they were too shook up to sleep, so they're watching something on the TV." He winked at me. "I think it has lasers in it."

"Told you." That was good. Ryan deserved a woman who had refined tastes. Lasers were awesome. Sitting, I wrapped my tail around my body. "Look, I've got to go soon. You think you can take care of them for me? Both of them?"

"I'll do my best." He gave a grave nod, then came to touch noses with me. "You're a good sort, Mystie. I wish we'd had more time to get to know each other, you know, when you were still breathing."

"Yeah, I think I would've gotten tired of your antics if we had." I twitched my whiskers. "You're an annoying whippersnapper. I like quiet."

"Sure." He smirked at me.

Yeah, Shawn would look after Ryan and Violet just fine. I bumped my forehead against his before ambling into the living room.

Ryan sat, one hand in the popcorn bowl on his lap, his other arm around Violet. Her head rested on his shoulder, and her eyes were closed. Sleeping? Well, she'd had a busy night. I settled on the couch and watched them until the movie credits rolled.

"Violet?" Ryan whispered.

She grunted but didn't move. With a slight chuckle, he eased out from under her then covered her with a fleece throw. After turning off the TV, he double checked the doors before stepping into the kitchen to watch the still munching Shawn. I hung back in the shadows, in spite of my desire to snap at Shawn for being a glutton ... as well how disrespectful it was for him to be devouring my kibble with such gusto so soon after my tragic demise.

"It's good to have a cat in the house again." Ryan's voice interrupted my thoughts. "Maybe I should go to the shelter tomorrow and have a look around." Shawn stopped eating and came to rub against Ryan's ankles. "You're a sweet boy." Ryan crouched to pet him. "Your owner's pretty sweet too. Do you think she likes me?"

Shawn started purring.

Ryan laughed. "Well, if she catches me talking to you like this, she'll probably think I'm nuts."

Somehow I knew Violet wasn't the type to judge him for that, but things seemed to be going pretty well so I kept quiet.

Ryan left the kitchen and walked down the hall to his bedroom. I could feel something tingling at the base of my spine. My tail quivered. Some instinct was pulling on me, wanting me to move on. The moonlight that had absorbed into my being tickled within me like the static energy that caused my fur to stand on end after rolling on the carpet.

But I had one last thing to do.

Drawing on my quickly fading energy, I gave out a meow. Ryan froze with his hand on the bedroom door, his face cloaked in shadows.

I focused with all my might on being seen, on being real. The moonlight coalesced within me until I started to glow like a star in the sky.

Ryan's jaw dropped. "M ... Mystie?"

I hurried towards him, leaving a trail of stardust in my wake. I rubbed against his legs. He reached down, his fingers tickling my glowing fur.

"Mystie," he whispered.

A low purr rumbled through me, and I gazed up at him with all the adoration he deserved. Then with a great leap, I bounded from the floor and through the ceiling. The moon beams caught me like the current of a river, and I found I could fly. Soaring through the stars like every bird that had ever escaped my claws. The horizon grew brighter, and I disappeared into it. Free and whole and happy.

My human would be all right.

As for me, I was ready for a new adventure.

The End

ABOUT H. L. Burke

Born in a small town in north central Oregon, H. L. Burke spent most of her childhood around trees and farm animals and always accompanied by a book. Growing up with epic heroes from Middle Earth and Narnia keeping her company, she also became an incurable romantic.

An addictive personality, she jumped from one fandom to another, being at times completely obsessed with various books, movies, or television series (Lord of the Rings, Star Wars, and Star Trek all took their turns), but she has grown to be what she considers a well-rounded connoisseur of geek culture.

Married to her high school crush who is now a US Marine, she has moved multiple times in her adult life but believes home is wherever her husband, two daughters, and pets are.

For information about H. L. Burke's latest novels, to sign up for the author's monthly newsletter, or to contact the writer, go to www.hlburkeauthor.com.

Also by H. L. Burke

FOR MIDDLE GRADE READERS
Thaddeus Whiskers and the Dragon
Cora and the Nurse Dragon
Spider Spell
Absolutely True Facts of the Pacific Tree Octopus

For Young Adult Readers
An Ordinary Knight
Beggar Magic
Coiled
Spice Bringer
The Heart of the Curiosity
Ashen

The Nyssa Glass Steampunk Series:
Nyssa Glass and the Caper Crisis
Nyssa Glass and the House of Mirrors
Nyssa Glass and the Juliet Dilemma
Nyssa Glass and the Cutpurse Kid
Nyssa Glass's Clockwork Christmas
Nyssa Glass and the Electric Heart

The Dragon and the Scholar Saga (1-4)
A Fantasy Romance Series
Dragon's Curse
Dragon's Debt
Dragon's Rival
Dragon's Bride
To Court a Queen

Ice and Fate Duology
Daughter of Sun, Bride of Ice
Prince of Stars, Son of Fate

The Green Princess: A Fantasy Romance Trilogy
Book One: Flower

Book Two: Fallow
Book Three: Flourish
Spellsmith and Carver Series
Spellsmith & Carver: Magicians' Rivalry
Spellsmith & Carver: Magicians' Trial
Spellsmith & Carver: Magicians' Reckoning
Fellowship of Fantasy Anthologies
Fantastic Creatures
Hall of Heroes
Mythical Doorways
Tales of Ever After
Paws, Claws, and Magic Tales
Match Cats: Three Tails of Love
Supervillain Rehabilitation Project Universe
Relapsed (a short story prequel)
Reformed
Redeemed
Reborn
Refined
Reunion
Blind Date with a Supervillain
On the Run with a Supervillain
Captured by a Supervillain
Engaged to a Supervillain
Accidentally a Supervillain
A Superhero for Christmas
A Superhero Ever After
Second Chance Superhero
Wishing on a Supervillain
Her Fake Superhero Boyfriend
Coming Soon: Rescuing a Supervillain
Power On

Power Play
Power Through
Power Up
Game On
The DOSA Files: Tales from the Supervillain Rehabilitation Project Universe